DOUBLE TROUBLE

A MATERNAL INSTINCTS MYSTERY

DIANA ORGAIN

OTHER TITLES BY DIANA ORGAIN

IN THE MATERNAL INSTINCTS MYSTERY SERIES

Bundle of Trouble

Motherhood is Murder

Formula for Murder

Nursing a Grudge

Pampered to Death

Killer Cravings

A Deathly Rattle

Rockabye Murder

Prams and Poison

Lethal Lullaby

Cereal Killer

Double Trouble

Murder comes Crawling (Coming soon)

IN THE IWITCH MYSTERY SERIES

A WITCH CALLED WANDA

I WANDA PUT A SPELL ON YOU

BREWING UP MURDER

IN THE GLUTEN-FREE MYSTERY SERIES

Murder as Sticky as Jam

Murder as Sweet as Honey

Murder as Savory as Biscuits

IN THE LOVE OR MONEY MYSTERY SERIES

A First Date with Death

A Second Chance at Murder

Third Time's a Crime

IN THE ROUNDUP CREW MYSTERY SERIES

Yappy Hour

Trigger Yappy

Double Trouble

A Maternal Instincts Mystery

---

by
Diana Orgain

CONTENTS

CHAPTER ONE

o-Do:

1. Throw Laurie’s birthday party.
2. ~~Organize pantry.~~
3. Repack hospital bag more efficiently.
4. Clean bathroom.
5. Fix crooked poster in nursery.
6. ~~Vacuum everything.~~
7. Vacuum everything again.
8. ~~Find a case?~~ No, not this month. No time.

“GIRL’S DAY!” shrieked my best friend Paula, clinking an imaginary champagne glass as the automatic doors opened in front of us. “Time for a shopping spree!”

I tugged at a red shopping cart nested inside another cart. “Well, the budget is exactly two hundred dollars, so I’m not sure how much room that’s going to leave for *spree*ing.”

The shopping cart didn’t budge. I grimaced and pulled harder.

Paula threw out her arms, looking far too fashionable in her belted teal shirtdress and brown ankle boots. “Conveniently, my friend, you happen to know an event planner extraordinaire. I can throw the world’s best first birthday party on even the most shoestring of budgets.”

Shoestring budget? I jerked, startled. *It's Laurie's first birthday party, not the Met Gala. Shouldn't two hundred dollars be enough? Am I . . . shortchanging my baby girl?*

Someone tapped my shoulder, and I waddle-pivoted to find an elderly Hispanic gentleman offering me a cart. "Here, *señora*," he said in a thick accent, his gaze flicking to my heavily pregnant belly. "For you."

I let out a little sigh of gratitude and accepted the cart. "Thank you."

I was almost thirty-six weeks pregnant with the twins, and a lot of everyday tasks weren't coming as easily as they used to. Gripping the handle, I leaned forward to let the cart bear the brunt of my extra weight and followed Paula into the store.

Our first stop: the crowded clearance aisle.

"We'll just see what we have here," said Paula, "before we wander over to the party section. Since we're keeping the budget modest, we want to stretch every dollar."

I bit my lip, a wave of guilt washing over me. *Should we have set aside a bigger budget for the party? Maybe I should call Jim, and we can agree on an extra hundred dollars?*

My husband was working from home with Laurie and Paula's two kids, but surely he had time for a quick phone call . . .

I shook my head and chided myself. *She's not even going to remember this party. She'll just be happy that she gets to smear chocolate cake all over her face. And our expenses are going to go way, way up when the twins are born.*

I pawed through the nearest rack, looking through the haphazard collection of scented candles, mermaid-print bandanas, and fidget toys. I picked up a patriotic-looking snow globe and squinted at the figure of George Washington in the center.

What in the world?

I shook it, and red-white-and-blue sparkles blizzarded around George Washington.

Leftover Fourth of July merchandise.

I snorted and set the snow globe back down, moving on to inspect a bin full of umbrellas emblazoned with phrases like "dance in puddles" and "rain waters my soul."

"There's not a whole lot of party stuff here," I called to Paula.

But my friend was bending over, digging deep into the bowels of a display rack.

Movement in the corner of the store caught my eye. I turned my head, glimpsing a collection of giant inflatables peering down at me from several aisles over—a witch with a cauldron, a stack of leering pumpkins, and a purple dragon.

My chest tightened. *That's right—Halloween's next month, and I still need to get Laurie a costume! And what about the twins? They're due in four short weeks!*

Dry panic flooded my mouth.

I'm never going to get everything done!

"Got it!" called Paula triumphantly. She waved a roll of yellow crepe streamers in the air. "In duck-yellow, just like Laurie's ducky-themed bedroom. And they're buy-one-get-one-free!"

"Oh, those are very pretty!" I exclaimed, but my gaze flicked back to the Halloween inflatables.

I didn't like the witch inflatable, I decided. She had a judgmental expression on her face—like she disapproved of my paltry party budget.

Or maybe she just knew that I'd never accomplish everything on my list.

"Should we go to the party section now?" I asked. "I'd like to get back home soon so I can vacuum."

Paula dropped the streamers into the cart and put her hands on her hips. "You vacuumed yesterday, Kate."

"So?" I shrugged nonchalantly, trying to play it casual. "We can't have it dusty at Laurie's party."

"And Jim said he couldn't stop you from organizing the pantry on Tuesday."

I frowned. "It was in dire need of organization. I think it hadn't been done in a whole year."

"A year," said Paula, overenunciating the words. "What happened a year ago?"

Ooooooooh. I pushed the cart forward a few steps, feeling sheepish. "Okay, so *maybe* I go into nesting mode in the last month of a pregnancy. Is that a crime? Should we call a detective?"

Paula's serious expression wavered, and she suppressed a giggle. "You *are* a detective. Wait—you don't have any cases on your plate right now, do you?"

I shook my head. "No. No way. The next few months are going to be crazy busy, and I can't take on any new cases. I told Galigani that already. He agrees. I deserve a little maternity leave."

Paula stood in front of the cart, her arms crossed. "Exactly! That's what I'm saying. You don't need to vacuum again—give yourself a break. Remember how you ended up on bedrest for the last week of your pregnancy with Laurie?"

With a scowl, I protested, "That was preeclampsia! It had absolutely nothing to do with overexerting myself nesting."

She studied me skeptically.

"In fact," I added, "Dr. Greene told me that staying active might even help me avoid preeclampsia bedrest."

"You and your facts." She turned away from me to riffle through another rack of clearance items. "But I'm still not going to let you cut short our girls' day so you can go *vacuum*. We have a party to plan!"

I fell silent, glancing up at the Halloween inflatables. That witch was definitely mocking me—there was an unmistakable gleam in her eyes. Her expression somehow reminded me of Sergeant Patrick McNearny, the homicide detective I often feuded with while solving murder cases.

I smirked quietly to myself. I wouldn't tell Sergeant McNearny that he reminded me of an inflatable witch. He might not appreciate the humor.

"Oh!" Paula whirled back toward me, holding up a roll of blue crepe streamer. "Your ultrasound! How did it go?"

Resting a hand on my baby bump, I said, "Dr. Greene said she was finally able to tell if they're boys or girls—"

"One of each?" Paula squealed, eyes shining. "That'll be so fun! Oh, you can dress them in little outfits that almost match, but with boy and girl flair for each, and—"

"I don't know that it's one of each," I interjected. "She didn't tell me. I'm dying to know, but Jim wants to be surprised."

Paula made a face. "I'll talk to him. He's crazy. We need to know." She set the blue streamer back on the shelf in a huff. "What if you have two little boys and a closet full of Laurie's pink onesies?"

I swallowed back a sudden surge of anxiety. "Laurie had a lot of neutral clothes when she was tiny," I said weakly.

But deep down, I knew Paula was right. If either of twins was a boy—and especially if *both* of them were boys—we'd be totally unprepared.

Newborns spit up on six outfits a day. And twins . . .

We'd be dressing them in pink frilly skirts by the end of the first week!

I glanced down at my purse in the cart, then unzipped it and pulled out a thin white envelope. "I had Dr. Greene write it down and put it in this envelope, just in case I could talk Jim into it. Should I open it? We could shop for baby clothes while we're here, and—"

Paula snatched the envelope from my hands. "I have a great idea!" she exclaimed. "Let's do a gender reveal at Laurie's birthday party! Everyone will be at your house, anyway. I'll handle all the details, and surprise you and Jim!"

My lips twitched.

I'm not so sure about this . . .

"But shouldn't this party be about Laurie?" I asked. "We'd be letting the new babies take center stage at her birthday celebration. I already feel like I'm not making a big enough deal about it by capping the budget at two hundred dollars."

Paula waved away my objection. "Laurie will be fine. She's not going to know the difference."

Well, that's true. I was just thinking that Laurie won't even remember this party . . . but still . . .

"I won't take no for an answer," said Paula firmly, turning on her heel and pointing to the left. "To the party aisle!"

After another moment of hesitation, I nodded and pushed the cart after Paula. It was always easier to cooperate with Paula's whims than to resist them.

Maybe if I cooperated, we'd get home sooner.

And then I can vacuum.

In my open purse, I spied a half-crumpled piece of paper. My newest to-do list. I smoothed it out, looking at everything I needed to do.

Party planning. *Focus on throwing Laurie a great first birthday.*

We turned onto the party aisle, and my eyes landed on the last item on my list—one I'd scratched out already: ~~*8. Find a new case?*~~ *No, not this month. No time.*

I nodded, satisfied with my decision. Even though part of me itched to put my detective skills to good use, the smarter part of my brain knew I should take a few weeks off.

Unless, of course, a case finds me . . .

CHAPTER TWO

"Ladies and gentlemen, boys and girls!" called Paula, standing on an upside-down bucket in my living room. "In *five* minutes, we're going to have the gender reveal for the twins! Everyone start thinking about making their way into the kitchen. David is arriving with the cakes any moment." She placed her hand dramatically over her chest. "I was starting to worry the bakery wasn't going to finish them in time!"

From across the room, I made mournful eye contact with Jim. Paula's idea for a gender reveal was a pair of cakes—cupcake-sized, I hoped—that she wanted Jim and I to smash into each other's faces like an enthusiastic bride and groom at a wedding reception.

The idea didn't *thrill* me . . . but Paula had been so enthusiastic, and it seemed easier to play along.

I was too pregnant to argue.

Our house was packed out with friends and family. My mom and her boyfriend Galigani sat on the couch in conversation with Jim's brother, George, and George's wife, Kiku, who was holding her little one. My dad and stepmom stood near the doorway to the kitchen with Deb, my policewoman friend. Laurie shuffled across the floor, chasing Paula's toddler son, and our poor cat Whiskers hid under one of the couches evading Paula's nine-month-old-daughter Chloe.

A knock sounded at the door, and I opened it to find my friend and rival PI, Vicente Domingo and his cousin Baramendi, with Sergeant McNearny a step behind them.

"Sorry we're late!" Baramendi said. "We were just wrapping up a few loose ends at work."

Vicente shrugged sheepishly. “Kate knows how it is,” he said. “Sometimes you just can’t break away from an important case.”

“Oh?” I raised an eyebrow, suddenly intrigued. “Anything I can help with?” I asked against all my better judgment.

McNearny scowled at me, though there was a grudging respect in his eyes. “Not a chance, Connolly. You’re on maternity leave, remember? Galigani said you told him yourself that you didn’t want any cases for a few weeks.”

“That’s right,” Galigani piped up from his position on the couch.

“I know, I know,” I grumbled, waving them inside. “I’m just not a hundred percent sure I meant it.”

Vicente chuckled, and the group joined us inside.

McNearny grumbled, “Connolly, with your uncanny sense of timing, there’ll probably be a murder in the hospital while you’re giving birth.”

From across the room, Deb yelled, “I heard that, Sergeant! Don’t you be giving Kate a hard time now.”

Just then, Rachelle—our new nanny—walked out of the kitchen, carrying two glasses of ice water. “Hi Uncle Patrick!” she called, waving cheerily at Sergeant McNearny.

The sergeant muttered something unintelligible in my general direction. He still wasn’t thrilled that I’d hired his niece as our nanny—but it seemed like he was *starting* to get used to the idea.

A shrill baby scream broke over the party noise. I whirled, my heart jolting to a gallop, to see Laurie sitting on her bottom in the middle of the living room, her face crumpled in a deep sob.

“Ooooh!” I cooed as I swooped toward her and eased myself to sit at her side. “What’s wrong, little duck? Don’t cry at your own birthday party, sweet girl!”

Laurie threw herself into my lap with a guttural sob.

“Oh, honey,” I murmured, stroking her back. “Did you fall down?”

Paula's three-year-old peeked out from behind Rachelle's legs, his wide-eyed expression giving him away.

I crossed my arms and trained a stern stare on him. "Danny," I called in a commanding voice. "Did you make her cry?"

Danny bit his lip, then took a small step forward and pulled a stuffed duck from behind his back. "Sorry, Laurie," he said, holding out the duck.

I accepted the duck from Danny and handed it to Laurie. She grabbed it and clutched it tightly to her chest.

"Oh, did he take your duck?" I asked. "See? He gave it back and said he's sorry. Can you say, 'I forgive you'?"

Laurie just studied Danny dourly, and I suppressed a snort. I hadn't expected Laurie to actually repeat the words, but her expression clearly communicated that she did *not* forgive him.

The door opened, but I ignored it, focusing on negotiating a peace between the two children. "Danny, can you—"

Someone jostled my arm, and I looked up sharply. My eyes widened. Paula's husband had arrived with the cakes. And . . .suddenly a delighted baby Chloe zipped across the floor to greet her father.

Oh no.

He was tripping, falling, windmilling his arms with panic in his eyes.

The world slowed down as the cake boxes flew toward the ceiling, flipping over in midair and dumping a pair of bigger-than-cupcake-sized white-frosted cakes directly above our heads. By instinct, I leaned forward, covering Laurie, protecting her from the oncoming frosting missiles.

"Nooooooo!" my sweet husband called, lunging toward us, arms outstretched. He made contact with one of the cakes face-first, knocking it off course.

A light shower of pink crumbs rained down around me. *A girl . . .*

Then the second cake hit my head, rattling my skull.

Laurie's whimpering sobs heightened to a shriek. I blinked, shaking off the cake, inspecting Laurie for injuries.

"Are you okay?" I asked in a soothing voice.

Much to my relief, Laurie was fine—a few flecks of frosting dotted her party dress, and one of her shoes was covered in pink crumbs, but she'd mostly avoided the disaster. My head pounded, and I reached up to touch my hair.

I was *covered* in cake.

I pulled my hand away, staring blankly at the white frosting and pink crumbs on my fingers.

Pink. Again.

Two pink cakes.

I blinked a few times, trying to process what had just happened.

"Two girls!" cried Jim.

I glanced from person to person. Jim was fist-pumping the air, a mask of cake coating his face and the front of his button-up shirt. Everyone else in the room was deathly silent and wide-eyed, every mouth covered by a hand.

I shifted Laurie onto my hip and reached up toward Jim. He leaned over and helped me to my feet. Laurie's shrieks returned to soft whimpers, and she reached for her daddy with a choked sob.

"Are you all right, honey?" Jim asked in concern.

"I'm just fine," I said, my hand drifting to my hair again. "A little bit of a headache, maybe. Are you all right?"

"I'm great!" he exclaimed. "We're having baby girls!"

I looked around the living room at the explosion of pink. "You're not disappointed that you're not having a son?"

"Not in the least. This is going to save us so much money." He fist-pumped the air and started chanting, "Hand-me-downs! Hand-me-downs!"

From the couch, my mom tittered, then burst into a fit of giggles. After a moment, Galigani followed suit, leaning forward with his face in his hands and chortling.

Then the whole party dissolved into laughter—everyone except Paula and her husband, whose faces had paled to the same shade as the vanilla frosting that now adorned my hair. David stood a few steps away from me, shaking. Paula was at his side, tears brimming in her eyes.

I grinned at them. "Well, this is certainly a gender reveal to remember!"

My mom crowed. "One we'll never forget!"

I waddled a couple of steps toward Paula. "It's a great party," I said in a reassuring voice.

A tear streamed down Paula's face. "I ruined it!" she cried. "I should have just gotten the cakes from the bakery at the grocery store, so we had them in place before the party started! We should never have tried to bring them in partway through, amid all the chaos."

A pang seized my midsection, and I sucked in a gasp, lurched backward, and grabbed Jim's arm.

"What is it?" Jim asked.

I let out a slow exhale, then carefully inhaled. *Breathe through it.*

Then the pang released me, and I let out a shaky laugh. "Just a Braxton Hicks contraction—I feel fine now."

Jim studied me in concern, but I waved it away.

"They're perfectly normal at this stage of pregnancy," I assured him. "I've already had a few this week."

I shuffled forward to grab Paula's hand. "Don't feel bad! You're going to see how hysterical this was in a week!"

I gestured at the other partygoers. My brother-in-law had fallen to the floor laughing, and tears of mirth streamed down Rachelle's face, smudging her mascara. She wiped the tears away, then broke into another fit of guffaws.

"See," I added, "best party ever—the guests are having a great time."

Paula managed a shaky smile. "I guess they are."

"Now," I said with a grin, "could you do us a favor and get Laurie changed into a new dress? Jim and I are both in *dire* need of a shower."

Paula nodded mournfully. "Let me rake the worst of that cake off your head and into the trash. We don't want to clog your drain."

CHAPTER THREE

The hot water felt absolutely heavenly on my pounding head.

Jim had chosen the guest bathroom, leaving the larger shower in our master for me. I took my time scrubbing away the remnants of the sticky frosting, secure in the knowledge that Paula would pull out all the stops to play hostess to our guests.

Another pang ricocheted through my abdomen, the sickening, tightening sensation hitting me like a piano falling out of the sky. I slammed one hand against the wall and grabbed at the shower curtain with the other. The fabric jolted, a ripping sound telling me I'd pulled the curtain halfway off the hooks. I staggered to keep my balance, leaning forward with both my palms pressed against the fiberglass.

Breathe in. Breathe out. Just a Braxton Hicks.

The seconds dragged on and on and on. Finally, the tightening sensation eased. I stood up straight, took a slow breath, and turned the knob to send a stream of cool water washing over me.

I couldn't be starting labor already, could I?

But I dismissed the treacherous thought by pure force of will. *The twins might come early, but not this early. We just have to get through this party and Laurie's birthday, and then the twins can make their debut anytime.*

Squinting at the drooping curtain, I half-considered trying to reattach it to the hooks, but decided against it. *I need to get back to Laurie's party. Jim will fix it later.*

I shoved aside folds of fabric, toweled off, and scrunched my hair mostly dry, then picked out a cute maternity dress that flattered my bump.

When I made my way back out to the party, my dad was sitting on the floor with Laurie, reading a board book to her. The other party guests milled around the living room and kitchen. When Jim saw me, he crossed the room and pulled me into an awkward over-the-bump hug.

"Feeling better?" he murmured in my ear.

"Much! Is Laurie having a good time?" I asked, standing on my tiptoes to peer over his shoulder at my baby girl on her grandpa's lap.

"She's having a great time," he said. "Her grandparents were positively fighting over her."

Galigani and Rhonda, my stepmom, walked out of the kitchen chatting and laughing. I smiled a little. I was glad everyone was starting to become friends. My dad had moved back to San Francisco a couple months earlier, eager to make up for lost time. While I'd been hesitant to accept his presence at first, it felt really nice to have a dad again.

But speaking of Laurie's grandparents . . .

"Where is my mom?" I asked.

Jim shrugged. "She left a few minutes ago."

"She left early?" I demanded, crossing my arms. "Her own granddaughter's first birthday party? Why? Is something wrong?"

"No, no. She said she'd be right back." He scratched the back of his neck. "You know how your mom gets. She was on a mission. She takes an idea into her head and runs after it like the bulls in Pamplona."

"*Olé*!" Vicente cheered from across the room upon overhearing the word Pamplona.

Truer words were never spoken. I chuckled. "Did she say what her mission was this time?"

He shook his head. "Nope. We were mid-conversation when her face lit up and she declared she'd be back in fifteen minutes." He glanced down at his watch. "Which means she should be back in ten or so?"

My dad set down the board book and stood up, swinging Laurie high into the air. She let out a shriek of high-pitched toddler giggles, and a warm feeling filled my chest.

I squeezed Jim's hand. "I'm so glad we're celebrating Laurie's birthday before the twins arrive—that she gets to be the complete center of attention on her special day."

Except that we had the twins' gender reveal and made her cry. Guilt—or acid reflux—burned my esophagus. I swallowed it back.

"Me too," said Jim. "Even if it is one day earlier than her *actual* birthday."

"Kate's back!" cried Paula from behind me.

I turned around with a grin. "Refreshed and ready for the rest of the party," I declared.

"Well, then," said Paula, "if you haven't already had too much cake, is it time to sing happy birthday to Laurie and let her eat her first piece of chocolate cake?"

Holding up a hand, I said, "Yes—almost. I guess my mom stepped out for a few minutes. We should wait for her."

Paula glanced up at the clock in the living room and nodded, a frown on her face. "We're behind schedule because of the disaster, but that's my fault—I'll make it work."

Where did Mom run off to? Annoyance coiled in my stomach. "If she's not back in fifteen minutes, we'll do it without her," I said. I walked over to the hooks by the door and grabbed my phone out of my purse. "I'll text her to let her know."

"Sounds good!" called Paula. "I'll push the big surprise back a few minutes."

Paula had been talking about *the big surprise* for a whole week.

"Is that too much trouble?" I asked, opening up my text messages with Mom.

She waved a hand. "It's not ideal, but it is what it is. I'm sure it'll be fine." With a half-sigh, she swept out of the living room into the kitchen.

I bit my lip and tapped out a text to Mom: *Can you come back now? We need to serve Laurie's cake.*

"I think this girl wants her mama!" called my dad.

I glanced up, and Dad handed Laurie to me. I tucked my phone in the dress pocket and took my baby girl. She cuddled up against me, and a wave of maternal feeling pulsed through my core.

And then I smelled it—the telltale stench of an especially gnarly poopy diaper.

I wrinkled my nose and locked eyes with my dad.

He shrugged, a twinkle in his eyes. "Oh, and I think she's got something in her diaper. You might want to take care of that."

"You don't say?" I replied with a laugh. "I'll change her and be right back."

Another contraction hit me, and I sucked in a gasp.

"Kate?" Dad asked, but it sounded like he was speaking through water. "Kate? Are you all right?"

I sank back a couple steps, and Dad took Laurie from me.

"Jim!" he called. "Jim, I think Kate might be in labor!"

"What?" gasped Deb, my policewoman friend. "Kate, do you need a ride to the hospital?"

"No. Fine," I hissed. "Just Braxton Hicks."

I sank back against the wall to steady myself, focusing on breathing in and out. When the contraction finally eased, I looked up to find the whole party staring at me. Jim stood at my side, resting a protective hand on my shoulder.

"Honey, are you in labor?" he asked.

"No," I exclaimed breathlessly, though doubt nibbled at my insides. My eyes rested on Laurie.

If I started labor *now,* the twins would be born *on* her birthday. She'd have to go the whole rest of her life sharing her birthday with her little sisters. That couldn't happen.

Which meant I couldn't be in labor. Not yet.

"I'm so sorry to alarm everyone," I said, trying to look as calm and unruffled as possible. "Braxton Hicks contractions get really strong. I need to change Laurie's diaper now."

I snatched Laurie from my dad and marched down the hall, determination flooding me with each step.

This isn't labor. I absolutely, positively am not going into labor.

I made faces at Laurie to make her giggle as I changed her diaper. By the time we rejoined the party, I felt normal again. Except my feet were killing me.

False alarm, thank goodness.

My phone buzzed in my pocket, and I sank down to sit on the couch with Laurie, then fished the phone out.

The message was from my mom: *Sorry, darling. Back in a jiffy!*

Laurie squirmed. I set her down on the carpet so she could run after little Danny.

The police contingent—Sergeant McNearny, Officer Deb, and Nick the medical examiner—approached and sat on the floor across from me.

"You good, Connolly?" McNearny asked.

Was that *concern* on his face? I cracked a grin. "Feeling great," I replied. "Well, as great as anyone feels while this pregnant."

"Can't be that great, then," deadpanned Deb, raising her can of beer in the air.

Nick's wife Denise sat on the couch next to me. "Can I get you anything?" she asked.

"You guys are so sweet," I said. "But really, I'm fine. I promise."

The door opened, and my mom hurried in, carrying two pink gift bags. "I'm baaaaack!" she sang. "I didn't miss the cake-cutting, did I?"

"You did not!" I said. "Shall we sing happy birthday?"

She held up the bags. "I just ran out to Baby Emporium to pick up a couple little gifts for the twins!"

My mouth fell open, and I stared at her.

But Mom continued on, seeming not to notice my abrupt shift in mood. "It's not every day you find out your daughter is having twin girls!"

"This is supposed to be Laurie's party," I said, "can we set the baby gifts aside to open later?"

Paula darted around the corner, waving a hand wildly. "Oh, good! Vera's here! Everyone come into the kitchen! I have Laurie's cake set up! We need to hurry!"

Denise helped me to my feet, and I followed everyone into the kitchen. My jaw dropped. Laurie's high chair sat by the kitchen counter, next to the fanciest birthday cake I'd ever seen.

Paula had outdone herself with this cake.

Three tiers of perfectly sculpted cake rose from a platter, each layer different. The bottom layer was cloaked in pastel piping, the icing in soft shades of pink and green and duck yellow. Sprinkles covered the middle layer, in a comparable color palette. The top tier was plain white, with chocolate drizzles melting down the sides and topped by a beautiful pink bow.

It looked more like a wedding cake than a first-birthday cake, except for the pastel colors.

"Ladies and gentlemen, let's give it up for the birthday girl, Miss Laurie!" cried Paula.

Everyone clapped and cheered, and Galigani gave a whooping yell.

My mom held up the gift bags and said, "I picked up a couple gifts for the twins. Where should I put them?"

I opened my mouth to object, but Paula pointed at the far end of the kitchen table and said, "Why don't you just set them there, with Laurie's birthday gifts?"

Can't this wait? I made eye contact with Jim, but he didn't seem perturbed.

Paula set a small portable speaker next to the cake and tapped her phone screen. The tune of "Happy Birthday," with a decidedly polka flair, poured out of the speaker.

Is that . . . accordion music?

"All together!" Paula cried.

On cue, the partygoers sang, "Happy birthday to you!"

Laurie raised her little hand high in the air and giggled, and I lifted my phone to snap a picture of her.

"Happy birthday to you!" everyone sang. "Happy biiiiirthday, dear Laurie! Happy birthday to you!"

We all clapped, and Laurie imitated us with a happy squeal. Paula cut the cake while I plopped Laurie in her high chair and gave her a high five.

"First piece for the birthday girl!" Paula cried, setting a small piece of chocolate cake, covered in sprinkles, on Laurie's tray.

Laurie's eyes widened as she stared at the delectable treat. She plunged her fist into the sprinkles and stuffed a handful in her mouth. Chocolate crumbs flew off the side of her tray.

Then it happened again.

My midsection convulsed and tightened. Another Braxton Hicks contraction.

I sucked in a sharp breath, then slowly exhaled, taking two steps back and sinking onto a dining chair.

As I leaned forward and breathed through the contraction, a simple refrain echoed in my head: *This isn't labor. This isn't labor. This isn't labor.*

I sensed someone's eyes on me, but I didn't look up. I just waited for the pain and pressure to ease.

This contraction seemed to last longer than the others had. A warning bell rang in my head, but I quieted it.

This isn't labor.

When it finally ceased, I let out a shaky breath and looked up. Most of the attendees were focused on Laurie, who was shoveling cake into her mouth like her life depended on it. But three people had noticed my contraction: Jim, my dad, and Denise.

Denise weaved through the crowd and sat in the chair next to mine. "This isn't normal, Kate," she whispered urgently. "You're in labor."

"I can't be in labor," I hissed. "Laurie's birthday is tomorrow. If the babies steal her birthday, she'll grow up resenting them!"

She scowled at me, but sisterly concern shone in her eyes. "The twins will have to share their birthday with each other no matter what," she said. "And they'll grow up used to that. If Laurie happens to share that birthday, too, she'll grow up used to it, too. You'll find ways to make it special for all of them."

Then another horrifying thought hit me. "My OBGYN is in Rome!" I exclaimed. "She doesn't get back until Tuesday! I can't have the babies without a doctor there."

"I'm sure there's more than one doctor at the hospital," she replied placidly. "Giving birth isn't usually something you can just reschedule to fit a doctor's vacation plans." With a crooked smile, she added, "Unless there have been some big advancements in modern medicine that I don't know about."

She was right. I groaned under my breath. *Why does she have to be right?*

But I was determined. Surely I could delay the inevitable by sheer force of will . . .

Just until Tuesday.

The doorbell rang, and Paula jolted.

"Did the duck not get my texts?" she hissed.

My forehead crinkled as I tried to make sense of that sentence. "The duck?" I asked. "What are you—"

But Paula had already whisked out of the kitchen. I tilted my head and tried to listen for her voice, but I couldn't make it out over the animated conversations going on around me.

A moment later, she reappeared. "It's time for Laurie's big surprise!"

Though I could tell Paula was stressed—we'd been best friends since we were kids, so I could read her like a book—she covered it up well.

Paula stepped aside, making way for the *big surprise.*

I covered my mouth to suppress a tittering laugh.

It was a duck.

The duck—a full-grown person in a big yellow duck costume—waddled into the kitchen, dragging a small wheeled cart.

"I hear there's a birthday duckling here!" the duck called in a baritone voice I recognized.

"Kenny?" I asked, locking eyes with the person in the costume. Sure enough it was my neighbor and Laurie's all-time favorite babysitter.

A chorus of tiny chirps caught my attention, and I glanced at the cart.

And gasped.

Kenny had brought a small flock of real, live ducklings! Into my house!

A moment later, my shock gave way to delight. What a perfect theme for Laurie's birthday party! "Awww, that's really cute," I exclaimed to Paula.

She beamed with pride. "I knew I had to make this party memorable."

Laurie, still fully intent on her cake, hadn't noticed the ducklings yet, so Jim reached over and patted her arm, then pointed at the cart of ducklings.

Then, movement eye caught my attention, and I gaped in horror.

Whiskers poked her head around the corner, her eyes hungry and curious, drawn in by the chirps.

Was Laurie's first birthday party about to be ruined by a great duckling massacre?

What trauma would she carry forward with her from such an event? I couldn't bear to contemplate it.

"Wait!" I yelled, waving my arms. "Take the ducklings outside! Whiskers!"

Kenny whirled in shock as Whiskers wiggled her little cat butt, preparing to pounce.

CHAPTER FOUR

"Nooooo!" I cried, stretching out my hands fruitlessly toward the poor, innocent ducklings.

"Nooooo!" Jim cried, running at Whiskers.

"Nooooo!" Kenny cried, throwing himself into a block worthy of a football linebacker.

For the second time that day, time slowed, and I saw every detail of the scene with startling, perfect clarity.

I couldn't reach the ducklings in time.

Jim bent down to scoop up Whiskers, grabbing her behind her front legs. Sweet relief prickled through me. Laurie's party was saved!

My relief was short-lived. Whiskers wriggled, practically morphing from solid to liquid and back to solid again before my eyes, squirming free of Jim and jumping at the ducklings.

But Kenny, off balance in the duck costume, was falling forward, still blocking Whiskers' access to the fluffy ducklings.

My breath caught in my throat. Startled, Whiskers parkoured off the costumed duck, back toward Jim, her claws scuttling on the floor as she darted back toward the hall.

Kenny hit the floor with a *thump*.

Shocked silence fell over the party.

Kenny scrambled to his hands and knees and gasped, "Out the back door. Before it comes back!"

"Good point!" Jim strode toward the back door and yanked it open, ushering Kenny in his duck costume and the cart of ducklings to safety.

I heard a sniffle and glanced toward the noise. Paula had burst into tears.

"What's the matter?" I asked.

She threw out her hands. "I've ruined the party! I can't seem to do anything right! First, the disastrous cake situation, and now this!"

Rachelle, our new nanny, put an arm around Paula's shoulders. "Everything's fine! The cat didn't make off with any ducklings. We'll just all go out to the yard, and Laurie can play with the ducklings there."

Paula sniffled, then looked at me.

Suppressing a giggle, I nodded solemnly. "You haven't ruined anything, Paula. And remember"—I shot her a grin—"you said you wanted to make this party memorable."

McNearny raised his red plastic cup toward Paula. "A toast! To the most memorable kid's birthday party I've ever been to!"

Nick and Denise chuckled, and Rachelle clinked her cup soundlessly against her uncle's.

"A toast!" replied Rachelle.

Paula still looked mortified, but she finally nodded. "Well, everyone," she said in a quavering attempt at a chipper voice. "Let's take this party outside!"

The guests filtered out to the backyard, and Paula and I stayed behind to get Laurie cleaned up.

I carried Laurie back to her duckie-themed bedroom, and Whiskers weaved between my legs as I pulled another dress out of the closet.

"Bad kitty," I said, though I'm sure my half-amused tone didn't at all get the point across to my mischievous little cat.

Whiskers purred back at me.

"I'm so sorry for losing it like that," Paula said from the doorway. "I've just been so emotional the last few days, and I don't know why."

I trained a sharp glance at my best friend. "Have you eaten anything today?"

She crossed her arms. "No, but I don't think I'm hangry. I've just been a little queasy."

Redressing Laurie, I asked, "Are you pregnant?"

Paula's forehead creased. "No! We've had our boy and girl. We're done. Surely I'm not . . ." She trailed off, as if unconvinced.

"Might want to take a test," I said with a grin. "Young moms are allowed some emotional swings, but since you're queasy, too . . ."

A contraction seized me, tightening my abdomen like a vise. I gripped the edge of the changing table and sucked in a breath through my teeth.

At once, Paula stood at my side, resting a soft hand on my upper back. "Breathe, Kate," she said. "Breathe through it. Keep breathing . . ."

This contraction seemed to take forever. I focused, trying to steady myself as I rode it out. By the time I finally let out a breath of relief, sweat beaded on my neck.

Paula crossed my arms and stared at me. "Kate."

"What?" I asked innocently, pushing away the treacherous truth.

"You're in labor."

"I can't be in labor," I said. "Because if I go into labor now, I'm going to have to leave Laurie's birthday party, and then the twins will probably end up being born on Laurie's actual *birthday*, and—"

"Rachelle and I will make sure Laurie has a great time at the rest of her birthday party," she said firmly. "I'm going to get Jim and tell him to take you to the hospital."

I chewed my lip and retorted, "I'll pick you up a pregnancy test on the way back."

"That might be a good idea," she grumbled, then disappeared into the hall.

I treasured the next couple of minutes I spent in the dim room, just staring at my baby girl. Laurie giggled and squirmed, making a face at me. She pushed herself to a sitting position and let out a little cry, holding out her arms.

"Do you want to be picked up, little duck?" I asked, scooping her off the table.

But she didn't want to be picked up. She squirmed again, and I set her on her feet on the floor, then groaned as I eased myself down to sit on the carpet.

She toddled to the bin of toys in the corner and pulled out a little stuffed bear, tossing it onto the floor. Then another bear. Then a stuffed cat.

"Booga!" she said, grabbing hold of a doll in a pink dress and throwing it to the ground.

"Booga!" I called back.

She turned to look at me, a huge grin on her face.

I thought my heart might explode outward from all the love building up in my chest. "Mama loves you so much. You know that? You know how much Mama loves you?"

She stumbled toward me, arms outstretched, and tackled me with a hug, her baby breath smelling of chocolate cake.

"That's right! Mama loves you so much. No one can ever take your place in my heart—even if the twins do steal your birthday," I said with a sigh.

"Kate?" Jim called, striding into the room. "Are you in labor?"

Laurie ran to her daddy and wrapped her arms around his legs.

I let out a half-sigh. "I still don't think so. Paula's pretty convinced, but—"

"You *really* don't think you're in labor, or you're determined not to be?" he asked, studying me seriously.

His sympathetic gaze melted me—I sure was tired of these pregnancy hormones making me feel like a marshmallow—and I squeaked, “I’m worried Laurie will resent the twins if they steal her birthday.”

He leaned against the doorframe. “It’s a birthday, Kate, not a stuffed animal. No one can steal a birthday. You can only *share* a birthday.”

I folded my hands tightly together. “I really don’t think I’m in labor.”

He laughed. “I’ll get the hospital bag, and let’s get you checked out. Do you need me to help you up?”

“Yes,” I grumbled.

He pulled me to my feet. “Besides,” he quipped. “If Laurie wakes up tomorrow to find two babies here, she’ll think they’re the best birthday present ever!”

CHAPTER FIVE

"How can I help you?" asked the young man sitting at the receptionist's desk.

The bright lights and sharp antiseptic smell gave the hospital a vaguely sterile feeling. For a moment, I stared at the man, trying to process what he was doing here. He was a little older than I'd thought at first, I decided—perhaps thirty or thirty-five, with a self-assured, friendly manner. All the receptionists I'd met here had been middle-aged women, and he looked distinctly out of place.

I'm not here to solve a case. So what if he doesn't fit the stereotype?

"She's in labor." Jim rested a hand on my back.

"Congratulations!" said the receptionist. I noticed a nametag—Samuel. "Is this your first?"

"Our second," Jim replied triumphantly. "Twins!"

"Well, let's get you back into a room as fast as we can, then," he said, tapping a few keys on his keyboard.

There was something I didn't like in his manner—something that came off as oily.

It doesn't matter—it's not like he's my doctor.

I held up a hand. "I really don't think I'm in labor yet, but I thought it was worth getting checked out. You can never be too careful with twins."

But by this point, even I knew my protests were probably futile. I'd had two contractions in the car—six minutes apart. A very good sign.

If I'd been hoping to go into labor.

Samuel nodded politely. "Well, we'll get you checked out and see if now's the time or if we can send you back home. Are you already a patient here?"

"Yesssssssss," I said, the word slurring into a hiss as an incoming contraction caught me off guard. I leaned forward, pressing my hands against the counter, and closed my eyes.

"Ma'am?" A note of impatience had entered Samuel's voice. "Was that a *yes*?"

Annoyance flared in my chest. Did he think I could just stop having a contraction so I could clearly answer his questions? How long had he worked in the maternity ward?

Jim spoke for me. "Yes, she's had her prenatal care with Dr. Greene."

"Mmm." He tapped a few more keys. "I'm sorry to say Dr. Greene's on vacation still. Do you think you could reschedule labor for next week?"

My eyes popped open.

But Samuel was smiling at me. "I'm just kidding. What's your name?"

I relaxed a little, but I was still annoyed by the joke.

"Kate Connolly," Jim said.

"How do you spell Connolly?"

Jim spelled my name and gave my date of birth and our license plate number.

I gritted my teeth, willing the contraction to end, willing this check-in process to end, willing this pregnancy to end.

Maybe it wouldn't be *so* bad if Laurie and the twins shared a birthday. It would mean that, in a few short hours, I'd finally be done being pregnant.

For the red of my life!

The contraction ended, and I let out another shaky breath.

If I'm lucky, maybe they'll even come before midnight . . . then the twins and Laurie would be Irish twins, less than one year apart!

"No changes in insurance?" Samuel asked. A young, pretty nurse in blue scrubs came through a door and stood a few paces away from Samuel, studying the computer screen.

"Nope," I said. "Same as last appointment."

"Great!" He stood and held out a hospital bracelet. "Let me put this on you, and Nurse Renee will take you back to triage."

The redheaded nurse offered a strained smile as Samuel put the bracelet on my wrist. "Hi, Kate. I'm Renee. Let's get you back to a room and get you checked out."

The printer spat out a piece of paper, and Nurse Renee clipped the sheet onto her clipboard without one glance at Samuel. "I'll be right out."

Were they ignoring each other on purpose?

Surely I'm imagining things. She's just trying to get me back to a room as quickly as possible.

She strode out the door with a practiced polish that assured me she'd done this a hundred times—a relief, since she looked younger than me.

A moment later, the door into the waiting room swung open, and Nurse Renee strode through, pushing a wheelchair.

I gratefully sank into it, and then we were off, gliding down the hallway under the fluorescent lights. Jim's shoes shuffled behind us, and I turned my head to call back to him.

"Honey, do you have my purse?"

"Yep! I have your purse and the hospital bag."

"Can you find my to-do list?"

Nurse Renee laughed out loud, her manner more relaxed than it had been at check-in. "Why don't you just set that list aside until we figure out if you're in labor or not? If the babies are coming, there's only *one* thing on your list, and that's giving birth."

She was right. I knew she was right. But my brain was stuttering on the list. What had I left undone?

"Jim?" I pleaded.

"Not a chance," he said. "Nurse's orders. The list doesn't matter."

My lashes fluttered closed, and I struggled to remember the list. *Throw Laurie's birthday party* had definitely been on it—item number one.

Check. Mostly. Between Laurie's grandparents, nanny, and honorary Auntie Paula, she'd have a great time at the rest of her party, even if I wasn't there for it.

What else was on the list? I never did vacuum again, but I guess I can let that go.

I hadn't repacked the hospital bag more efficiently! My eyes flew open in horror. What if I really was in labor, and we couldn't find the Chapstick when I needed it?

Then Jim will have Paula go pick some up and bring it to me. I steeled myself.

Then my hand flew to my mouth. "The poster!" I exclaimed. "On the wall in the twins' nursery. It's still crooked!"

Nurse Renee patted my shoulder indulgently and wheeled me into the triage room. "Easy does it," she murmured, helping me out of the wheelchair and onto the table. "Your husband will fix that poster when you get home, and you won't even be thinking about it when the babies are born."

I knew it was irrational, but I couldn't get that stupid poster out of my head. It was crooked. It was *wrong*.

The twins' nursery wouldn't be perfect when we brought them home!

She hooked me up to the monitors, and I settled in to await her verdict. Another contraction hit me, and I managed a glance up at the clock.

Five minutes after the last one.

Twenty minutes later, the contractions were coming every five minutes.

"Well, you're four centimeters dilated," said Nurse Renee. "And your contractions are regular. So, you're definitely in labor. I'm going to admit you, but you might be here a little while before the twins make their debut. Sound okay?"

"What if I say it doesn't sound okay?" I quipped.

She chuckled. "Well, I'd say you don't have too many other options right now. We want to be extra careful with twins."

"I was hoping to delay it until Dr. Greene got back from Europe," I said wistfully.

"Dr. Phillips will keep you safe and sound," she said in a reassuring tone. Then her voice dropped to a conspiratorial whisper, "He's kinda cute, too."

The blood drained from my face. "He?" I asked, grimacing.

I didn't want a male doctor for an OBGYN—and I especially didn't want to hear that the doc overseeing this deeply intimate process was *kinda cute.*

"Let's get you transferred back to a labor-and-delivery room," she said, "you'll need to be in the wheelchair for that, but once I get you settled in, we'll let your hubby help you walk the halls during early labor, so you're more comfortable."

She wheeled me back to the labor-and-delivery room, and I was relieved at the immediate change in atmosphere. Instead of the sterile lights of the hallway, this room was more dimly lit, with comfortable, subdued furniture.

After only about two minutes, the doctor came in.

"Hi Kate," he said with a friendly nod. "I'm Docta C, and I'll be attending to you today."

"Docta C?" I asked, confused.

This had to be the same doctor that Nurse Renee had mentioned—how many uncomfortably young, uncomfortably handsome OBGYNs could there be on duty in the maternity ward today?—but I'd thought she'd called him Dr. Phillips.

He reached out and shook my hand. "Dr. Cory Phillips, and I'll make sure you and the twins get through this with flying colors. Up front, how do you feel about C-sections?"

"I don't want one," I said flatly.

Jim pulled out a small binder from the hospital bag. "I have her birth plan here."

Docta C acknowledged Jim with a nod, then looked back at me. "Most of that is probably in your chart already," he said, stepping up to the computer and entering a password.

He pulled up my chart and hummed under his breath, almost like he was disappointed. "Looks like you want to do a vaginal delivery with an epidural, like last time?"

"That's right."

My mind raced. What else in the birth plan did the doctor need to know about at this stage? Jim could set up the Bluetooth speaker and my birthing playlist. "Could we get a birthing stool for labor? And dim the lights in here a little more?"

"Sure, sure," he said absentmindedly. "Let the nurse know next time she pops in, and she'll take care of all that. Call button is on the wall—don't hesitate to call her in if there's an emergency or the contractions suddenly start coming really close together."

With that, he swept out of the room, his white coat almost billowing behind him.

I bit down on my tongue. I didn't like this *Docta C* nearly as much as Doctor Greene, who exuded quiet, compassionate professionalism and keen attention to every detail.

But then another contraction hit me—along with this undeniable reality: the babies didn't care who the OBGYN on duty was.

When the contraction eased, I said, "Jim, can you make sure you can find the Chapstick in the bag?"

Jim eagerly complied, handing me a small tube of lip balm.

My lips weren't dry yet, but I used the Chapstick anyway, then asked Jim to help me stand up.

The photo session! I forgot to schedule the family photo session for next week! How could I have missed that?

I closed my eyes and tried to picture my to-do list. My jaw dropped.

I forgot to add it to the list!

"Let's walk the halls," I said. "And can you bring my phone? I want to call Mom and ask her to level that poster in the twins' nursery and schedule the family photo session I've been talking about."

He grabbed my phone and helped me to my feet. "I'm sure she'll appreciate an update," he said dryly. "So she knows that the twins really are coming. And we need to tell Rachelle that you're being admitted and that she'll need to stay with Laurie overnight."

The number of details frazzled me. I couldn't keep track of all of this. I wasn't prepared to be in labor! This was too soon!

My heart pounded faster, throwing me into a mini-panic attack.

Jim looped his arm through mine, and I calmed a little at his soothing, steady presence beside me. Whatever we went through in life, however unprepared . . . we always did it together.

We walked into the hall, and he dialed my mom on speakerphone.

"Darling!" Mom cried. "What's happening? Are you in labor?"

"They're admitting me," I said. "But I'm not in active labor yet."

"I'll be down right away," she replied. "Rachelle!" Her voice got a little quieter, like she'd pulled the phone away from her mouth. "Kate's in labor! Looks like you're on call to stay with Laurie tonight."

I took a step forward, and a contraction hit me. I grimaced, grinding to a halt.

Somehow, over the wave of pain and pressure, I heard Jim saying, "Kate wanted to know if you could schedule a family photo session for some time after the twins are born."

"Of course," Mom said. "When do you want it done, Kate?"

I couldn't reply—couldn't think of any specific answer to that question.

Jim said, "She's in a contraction right now . . . I don't have any idea. You had two babies—can you just take your best guess of when she'll be up to a photoshoot?"

The contraction built in strength, and I gripped Jim for support.

"Absolutely," said Mom. "I'll do that and head on over."

"Thanks so much, Vera!" Jim hung up and held me until the contraction eased.

"The poster!" I exclaimed breathlessly. "We forgot to tell her about the poster."

"Oh!" He slapped his forehead. "That was the thing you were so concerned about. I'll call her back."

But the call went straight to voicemail.

"I'll try her again in a few minutes," he said in a soothing voice. "And if we can't get through, I'll get Rachelle to do it later. The nursery will be perfect before we bring the twins home. I promise."

CHAPTER SIX

It felt like we walked the hallway forever—up and down, up and down, up and down. The contractions were four minutes apart, now, but when Docta C came back to check on me, I was only dilated to five centimeters. So, back to the hallway we went.

"You're doing great!" a woman exclaimed when we reached the far end.

I opened my eyes, surprised at the voice. "Thank you."

She wore the green scrubs of the hospital's orderlies and was pushing a cart down the hall.

"This part is hard, but very soon, you'll have your baby in your arms"—she pumped the air with her fist—"and all this will fade away from your mind. It'll be so worth it. The most beautiful thing in the world."

I managed a wan smile. "Babies. There's two of them!"

She gasped with excitement. "Twins! I love twins. Two precious little babies making their appearance—and labor's way less complicated than with triplets. Who's your doctor?"

"Well, normally it's Dr. Greene, but today I guess it's Dr. Phillips."

She pursed her lips like she'd tasted something sour. "Well," she said to Jim. "Make sure that little boy doctor takes good care of your wife."

Jim tilted his head. "What's that supposed to mean?"

She shrugged. "That sounded harsher than I meant it, I guess. He's a decent man and a decent doctor—I just think he doesn't always . . . know what's best for women in labor. Make sure you advocate for your wife's needs." Then her mood shifted, and she smiled again. "But don't you worry, dear. Soon you'll have your precious twins. Oh! I really think twins are the very best."

"Do you have twins?" I asked.

She shook her head, eyes suddenly a little sad. "No, I don't have children, but I used to be a doula here."

I tilted my head. "They have doulas here?"

"*Used* to have doulas," she said. "That stopped about . . . three months ago."

My jaw dropped. "They demoted you from doula to—"

"Nothing wrong with being an orderly." She rested her hands on the cart handle. "It's honest work. But you're right—it's an odd job for someone who's passionate about helping mamas bring babies into the world. I won't be here forever—I'm applying to other hospitals now. Might start my own business, even." Then she waved her words away. "But I'm rambling all about me, and this day is about you and your babies. Just remember—you're doing great, and your body already knows everything it needs to in order to bring those babies safely into the world."

She pushed her cart away, and I called after her, "Wait! What was your name?"

She turned around. "I'm Mama Tina, and I hope you have a wonderful, easy, breezy delivery."

We let Mama Tina return to her duties and walked back up the hall.

"That's too bad they discontinued the doula program," I murmured. "Someone with her warmth and passion shouldn't be forced out of her career like that."

"She'll get another job soon," he said. "She must have agreed to stay on as an orderly so that she could still be in the maternity ward and have conversations with moms in labor. She lit up when she saw you."

Another contraction hit, nearly doubling me over. When I recovered, I gritted my teeth and said, "They're getting worse. I need that epidural *now*."

Jim brought me over to the hospital bed, and I sank down to sit on it while he pressed the call button to summon Nurse Renee.

Would that picture in the nursery get straightened out before we got home? Why hadn't I fixed it myself when I'd noticed it was crooked?

Oh yeah, because I couldn't reach it over this mammoth baby bump.

I'd remind Jim to call mom again once I got the epidural.

At least I don't have a case to think about.

A moment later, Nurse Renee appeared. "Yes, my dear?"

"Could I get the epidural now? The contractions are getting really bad."

She frowned. "Let me see how dilated you are."

After another check, she shook her head. "Not yet, I'm afraid. We've got to wait a bit on that."

Desperation filled me, and I sat bolt upright. "But I *need* it!"

She pressed her lips together. "I'm sorry—you have to wait. Why don't you practice the deep breathing you learned in your birthing classes? That's carried women through natural childbirth for thousands of years."

Jim, apparently taking to heart Mama Tina's warning to advocate for me, interjected, "But it's not a thousand years ago—we have modern medicine for a reason. If my wife says she needs the epidural, she needs the epidural!"

"Sir," said Nurse Renee in a clipped voice, "do you want your wife's labor to stall out so that she needs a C-section? That's what happens if she gets an epidural too early."

I furrowed my brow at her. "That's outdated," I protested. "I read a study about this—early epidurals don't have anything to do with whether you'll need a C-section."

She gave me a pitying, somewhat condescending look, and all my appreciation for her evaporated.

"I've been working here long enough to have seen some patterns," she said. "And so has Docta C. He won't authorize an epidural until you're further along in labor."

"But what's the point of it if I don't get it until I'm practically pushing?" I asked, desperation lacing my voice.

"I really am sorry," she said, although she didn't sound sorry.

When she left, I looked at Jim, bewildered. "Dr. Greene gave me an epidural when I asked for it."

"I don't like this birthing team nearly as much as the last one," Jim muttered. "This must be what Mama Tina was talking about when she said Docta C doesn't always know what birthing moms need. I'm going to go find him and—"

"Don't leave me!" I clutched his hand. "We'll reason with him when he comes to check on us."

Contraction by contraction, I white-knuckled through early labor. At some point, my mom arrived, and then a new nurse swept in. She had purple-rimmed glasses and an intense expression, giving off the air of someone who should be wearing a flower-power necklace.

"Hi, I'm Bindi," the nurse declared. "I'm one of the NICU nurses, and I wanted to introduce myself before the babies are born."

"NICU?" I asked, startled. "I'm at thirty-six weeks. They shouldn't need to go to the NICU!"

"Hopefully not," said Nurse Bindi, "but I'll be here after they're born, just in case. We'll put them through some tests and make sure that they're able to go home with you." She rested a hand on my arm and said, "They'll probably pass with flying colors."

One more thing to worry about. Emotions welled in my chest and tears burned my eyes.

Jim watching my face closely, mistook my emotion for pain and asked, “Any chance of getting my wife an epidural?”

Nurse Bindi paused, sympathy flashing across her features, then said, “That’s not really my area, but I’ll let the doctor know you want to talk about epidural timing, all right?”

“Good enough,” I said lightly, even though I wanted to snap, *Can’t you see I’m suffering here? Give me the darn epidural!*

She paused in the doorway and turned back to look at us. “Don’t worry about the babies, my dear. They probably won’t need to go to NICU, and if they do end up there, I’ll move heaven and earth to keep them safe and healthy and get them ready to go back home with you real soon. Deal?”

I managed a smile, though her sudden intensity startled me. “Thanks, Nurse Bindi.”

When she left, Mom put her hand on my sweaty face. “Hang in there, darling.”

Jim called my mom over, and they conferred in quiet tones in the corner. I strained to hear what they were saying—the few words I could make out suggested they were conspiring to get me an epidural.

Then a pair of angry voices in the hall caught my attention.

I could just barely make out a woman’s voice—Nurse Bindi, I thought—saying, “Cory, I swear on my great-uncle’s grave, you’re going to burn in hell for all the wreckage you leave in your wake. You and Samuel both. I’m sick of looking at you!”

In a tone thick with contempt, Docta C replied, “What, can your crystals tell you who needs an epidural and who doesn’t? I swear on *your* great-uncle’s grave, next mistake *you* make here? You’re gone.”

"Not if you make your next mistake first—and we both know you will."

CHAPTER SEVEN

I grimaced, my heart pounding faster. Ordinarily, I'd be half-thrilled by such a juicy conversation, wondering if it might point to a case. What wreckage *had* Docta C left in his wake? Had someone died? How was Samuel involved? Wasn't that the name of the *receptionist*?

None of it made sense, and I loved solving puzzles.

But at this moment in time, I was less focused on solving puzzles than on birthing my twins safely—and I didn't like the implication that my doctor might be less than competent.

Not one little bit.

Docta C strode into the room, muttering under his breath, and I forced a neutral expression onto my face, pretending I hadn't overheard the conversation.

"I need an epidural!" I called.

But Nurse Renee had been right—Docta C didn't approve me for an epidural.

Not for another. Three. Hours.

By the time I finally got the pain block, I was ready to toss this upstart baby-faced doctor into the San Francisco Bay myself and give birth with just the nurses and that doula-turned-orderly helping me.

But once the epidural finally took effect, I let out a long sigh of relief.

"Smooth sailing from here!" declared Nurse Renee when she came in to check on me yet again. "I think you're getting close."

I glanced up at the digital clock on the wall, and tears sprang to my eyes. Its harsh red letters declared 11:44. We weren't even to the pushing stage yet, which meant that the twins were definitely going to be delivered on Laurie's birthday.

My reaction surprised me—I'd thought I'd accepted it already—but I realized I'd harbored the wild hope that my labor would progress quickly and that the babies would be born before midnight.

But I hadn't done well enough.

That's irrational. I can't make labor go faster by sheer force of will. Babies come on their own schedule.

Still, I couldn't shake the feeling. Had I failed in my first action as the twins' mother?

Another contraction. Mom wiped sweat off my forehead with a damp cloth.

A few minutes later, Paula walked into the room carrying a pair of pink balloons and two care baskets. Mom jumped up from her chair next to my stool and ran to take the gifts from her.

"Are you hanging in there?" Paula asked sympathetically.

I let out a shaky laugh. "Well, now that the epidural's kicked in, a lot better. I was a mess a half hour ago."

Paula flashed me a wicked grin. "I heard, why do you think I waited to come see you?"

I narrowed my eyes at her. "Yeah, right. You were no better."

She pursed her lips. "I swear, if I ever have another baby, I'm just going to do one of those hippie water births at home."

I snorted out loud.

She looked almost offended. "What? The doctors take forever to give you the epidural. By the time you get it, labor's almost over. And then, after you've had the baby, good luck breaking out of hospital jail if they decide they want to *monitor* you."

I smirked. "Do you remember that time I took you to the hospital when you thought you were in labor with Chloe?"

"Vaguely," she replied, tossing her hair. "All that stuff is kind of a blur."

"The first words out of your mouth were, 'When can I get that epidural?' Literally."

She crossed her arms and leaned back against the wall. "I don't think you're quoting me *exactly*."

"Maybe not, but I'm pretty close. You got downright combative when I asked if you wanted me to play you a meditation CD."

She shrugged, her eyes alight with amusement. "Okay, maybe I don't really want a hippie water birth."

"I might be ready for one after this experience," I muttered. "Dr. Greene was great, but I don't have a lot of confidence in this substitute teacher."

"Oh, why?" she asked, her brows furrowing. "I don't like the sound of that."

Mom and Jim shared a long look, but before I could answer, Docta C strode in.

"All right, let's get you checked out," he declared with the bedside manner of a disinterested cat.

Paula raised her eyebrows at me.

Docta C finished the exam and let out an excited whoop.

I stared at him, aghast.

"Fully dilated!" he called, reaching over and tapping the nurse call button with a dramatic flourish. "You're in active labor."

Paula crossed the room to squeeze my shoulder. "Weird vibe, huh?" she murmured so only I could hear.

I agreed with her, but I tried to put it out of my mind. I didn't want to think about weird vibes from my doctor while I was giving birth.

Oh, why did Dr. Greene go to Rome?

In a louder voice, Paula said, "I'll get out of here so there's not too much chaos, but just know that your mom and Rachelle and I are going to make sure Laurie's actual first birthday is *so* much fun. She'll have a great day."

"That's right!" declared Mom. "It'll be the best birthday ever."

"Thank you!" I squeezed Paula's hand, and she left.

Another contraction. I gasped. Sometime during that contraction, Nurse Renee entered the room.

When the contraction ended, she checked my blood pressure and called out, "Hey, doc? Her blood pressure is borderline high, even accounting for the strain of labor."

Docta C furrowed his eyebrows, then skimmed through my chart. "Mmm, history of preeclampsia?"

"That's right," I replied. "I was on bed rest with my first pregnancy."

"Well, we'll be a little cautious here, then. Let's get an ultrasound really fast. Renee, would you mind keeping an eye on her vitals for a few minutes?"

Is something wrong? Think happy thoughts. Don't transfer anxiety to the twins. So instead of watching Docta C's face, I tried to watch the babies on the ultrasound monitor. It was turned so that I couldn't clearly see it, but I caught glimmers of movement on the screen.

My heart melted. My babies! They were almost here!

"Breech," said Docta C, a tight expression on his face.

He glanced between Jim and me, brusque and businesslike. "Listen, I know you were planning a vaginal delivery, but with one twin breech and your blood pressure going up, we're going to have to do a C-section."

My mom shrieked.

I bit my lip and shook my head. "Isn't there any way to avoid that?"

"We could try," he said impatiently, "if you want to roll the dice on having a stroke."

I locked eyes with Jim. His face had blanched the shade of new-fallen snow. The poor man looked like he might be about to faint.

Nurse Renee interjected, "What the doctor means to say is that—"

"The doctor means to say exactly what he said," grumbled Docta C.

In a firmer tone, Nurse Renee said, "What the doctor *means* to say is that the risks of a natural delivery outweigh the benefits at this point. We strongly advise a C-section." Her face took on a compassionate cast, and her voice got a little husky as she added, "Your babies need you, Kate."

I bit down on my lip. "I don't really have a choice then, do I?" I said softly. I'd do whatever it took to be there for my babies. No matter what. I steeled myself. "Do it."

CHAPTER EIGHT

I don't know what I'd expected the C-section to be like, but I didn't feel a thing. I didn't see a thing, either—not with the sheet draped under my chin.

Jim didn't see a thing, either.

Not after he turned from pale to green and pitched over sideways, at least.

"Jim!" Mom and I screeched in unison when he hit the floor.

Nurse Renee chuckled. "He's not the first new dad to pass out like that. Dr. Phillips, do you have everything under control? I'll go find an orderly to help Mr. Connolly here, if that's all right."

"Go on," said Docta C in a disinterested tone, as if he hadn't even bothered to listen to what she had to say.

Nurse Renee swept out of the room, and Docta C continued with the C-section in wordless concentration.

Perhaps a minute later, a shattering scream from outside the room cut through the flurry of activity. My eyes popped wide, and Docta C's head jerked up. He met my gaze, then shrugged and returned to the C-section.

"That was awfully loud," he said. "Must be a first-time mom."

But my heart was already sinking into my stomach, and my detective mind flared to life. That hadn't sounded like the scream of a woman in labor.

It had sounded like a scream of fright—from an older woman.

My gaze flicked to Mom, clutching my hand, her eyes fixed on me with serene determination. "You've got this, baby girl," she said. "Just a little longer."

But she misunderstood my sudden turmoil. I wasn't distressed about the C-section.

I was distressed about that scream.

Had the hospital just lost a woman in childbirth? Had her mother been sitting at her bedside, just as my mother sat at mine?

Another scream. This time, Mom looked alarmed, too.

Then, a flurry of commotion sounded from the hall. Yells. Footsteps. I craned my neck, as if that would help me see through the windowless door to the sterile hall beyond.

"Please hold still," said Docta C, annoyance in his tone. "I have to be precise with this."

A minute later, all thoughts of the commotion outside flew from my mind at the sound of a perfect baby wail.

Warmth filled my heart. *My baby!*

"It's a boy!" called Docta C jubilantly.

My mind stuttered, tried to process what he'd just said. "A boy?" I asked, my brows furrowing.

"That's right . . ." He glanced toward the door. "Where on earth did Renee go?"

"To get an orderly," said Mom, pointing to Jim, who was still laid out on the floor.

"Ah," said Docta C. He grabbed for a towel, wrapped the baby in it and handed him off to my mom. "Hold him while I get the other one out."

Mom glowed. She gingerly accepted the most precious, tiny, perfect angel from the doctor, and brought him over to me. He was still covered in goo and bellowing fierce wails.

"He's perfect!" I exclaimed, tears filling my eyes. I reached out to caress his forehead, everything in me screaming to hold him.

"Please hold still," said Docta C.

I willed myself to be patient and just stared at my new son, at every perfect curve of his face.

The door opened and closed, and Nurse Renee came in with an orderly and a gurney in tow.

Together, they heaved Jim up onto the gurney and pushed him against the wall. I glanced up from my beautiful son for just a moment, and my heart plummeted again.

Something was very, very wrong.

Nurse Renee looked absolutely shattered.

"What is it?" I called.

She shook her head fiercely and forced a smile. "Nothing!" she said in a too-cheery voice. "Everything's fine!"

She took her place at Docta C's side and, moments later, the doctor declared, "Another boy!"

Jim sat bolt upright in the gurney, rubbing his head. "Another boy?" he asked faintly.

Nurse Renee rubbed the second baby off with a towel and brought him over to Jim.

"Meet your son," she said.

"My son . . ." Jim murmured, a look of wonder on his face. "I have a son!" He took the towel-wrapped baby and held him close. He met my gaze, his face shining. "We have a son!"

The door opened again, and Nurse Bindi hurried in. Though her manner was brusque and businesslike, she couldn't hide the distress on her face.

Something terrible had happened.

"Did someone die?" I blurted, remembering that fearful scream, unable to suppress a picture of a woman lying still and pale on a hospital bed, her mother weeping at her side.

Both nurses jumped, visibly startled.

"How did you know?" demanded Renee.

"The scream . . . it sounded like . . ."

Bindi took the baby from Jim, wrapping him tightly in a swaddle. "Don't worry, my dear. The police are already on their way, and security is already on site. We're all perfectly safe. Let's get these babies to the NICU to get them checked out."

I stared at her, my mind circling on her words. *The police. Security. We're all perfectly safe.*

Someone had died. But not in childbirth.

I gasped as the full meaning hit me. "There was a murder!"

CHAPTER NINE

"A murder?" exclaimed Docta C, standing straight up and whirling toward the nurses. "What the hell?"

My mom squeezed my hand tightly, and I stared at her and mouthed, "Don't say a word."

Nurse Renee's jaw tightened, and she nodded back toward me. "Finish sewing her back up," she said stiffly. "We have a job to do. The patients need us."

I watched his profile as he studied her, and his face softened. "It was Samuel, wasn't it?" he asked softly.

A shudder ran through her, and she said through gritted teeth, "Do your job."

He let out a hiss but quickly recovered himself.

The emotions ran through me so quickly I couldn't separate them.

I have twin sons. They're going to the NICU to get checked out. I had to have a C-section. Someone was murdered. Samuel—the front desk receptionist. I talked to him just a few hours ago.

McNearny's gruff comment at the birthday party flashed through my head. *Connolly, with your uncanny sense of timing, there'll probably be a murder in the hospital while you're giving birth.*

"But I'm on maternity leave," I whispered under my breath.

"What was that?" asked Docta C.

"Nothing," I said louder, gritting my teeth.

I'm literally getting stitched up after a C-section. This is the most "on maternity leave" I can possibly be.

My mind went to my newborn babies.

Well, it wasn't so much that my mind *went* to them. They were always there, always at the forefront of my thoughts, like a song I couldn't get out of my head, but more overwhelming, like they were at the center of everything.

My babies.

I can't take a case while they're in the NICU. I have to be here—I have to stay focused on bonding with them.

I bit my lip, then continued my line of reasoning. *The police managed before I became a private investigator, didn't they? There's no reason they need my help on every single case.*

But this case *had* landed on my doorstep. I'd spoken to the victim shortly before he was killed, along with a number of other people present in the maternity ward. Surely that gave me a leg up.

I'll speak to the police when they arrive, at least, and tell them everything I know.

Which meant I should learn as much as possible before they arrived.

I wondered if McNearny would head up this homicide investigation, if I'd get a gruff "I told you so" when I gave my statement to the cops. I hoped not. I liked McNearny—we'd developed a grudging respect for each other over the last year—but I felt too tired to put up with his attitude.

Labor is hard work.

I glanced up at Nurse Renee. "I'm so sorry about Samuel," I said, my voice huskier than normal. "He checked us in at the front desk."

She looked startled for a moment, then blinked back a sudden well of tears. "It's nothing you need to worry about."

"Were you close?" I asked, modulating my tone to be approachable, to try to coax her to open up. My mind flitted back to the strange distance I'd sensed between them at check-in.

Our eyes met, and I could see the war in her mind—the struggle between what was professional and what felt right in the moment.

Docta C muttered, "He was her ex."

I sucked in a sharp breath. "Oh."

Was Renee in the room when we heard the screams? Alarm bells rang in my head, and I tried to visualize the moment.

No, she'd stepped out, because Jim had fainted. She'd gone to find an orderly.

Which, from my perspective, gave her opportunity. And the fact that her ex had been killed? That gave her a whole range of potential motives.

We'll have to see what the security cameras show, I cautioned myself.

Still, I tensed up a little at the thought that a murderer might have attended the twins' birth.

Am I a bad mom? I brought my babies to a crime scene while they were being born!

I chased the thought away. *Don't be silly. This could have happened to anyone. I had no way to know there would be a murder here. I just . . . happen to be a murder magnet, apparently.*

"That must be so hard," I said softly, making eye contact with Renee. "How long ago did you break up?"

Her lip quivered, and the words tumbled out like the breaking of a dam. "Four months ago, after he lost his license."

"Lost his license? Was he driving drunk?" I knew the question was insensitive under the circumstances, but I had to press—just in case she'd tell me something she wouldn't tell the police.

"His medical license," said Docta C tersely. "And we're done! You're all sewn up."

"When can I see my babies?" I blurted.

Nurse Renee tucked a sweaty strand of hair behind my ear. “We’ll get you into a wheelchair and into the NICU as soon as we can, but we have to keep an eye on you for a little bit first, okay?”

“Jim!” I exclaimed, searching the room for my husband, suddenly aware he wasn’t with me. “Where did Jim go? And my mom!”

Nurse Renee said, “They went with Bindi—they’re with the babies in the NICU.”

That set my mind at ease. At least our little boys—*boys!*—would have one parent with them in their first few hours of life.

“Can he hold them in NICU?” I asked plaintively.

“Yes, of course,” crooned Renee. “That early touch is very important for them. Bindi makes sure that parents get as much touch time with the preemies as possible.”

The babies will be just fine. Jim and the nurses will take good care of them.

With that worry assuaged, my mind turned back to the murder.

Bindi! That argument with Docta C . . . she’d said both he and Samuel would burn in hell and that she was sick of looking at them.

And Docta C had said Samuel had lost his *medical license*. So, Samuel used to be a doctor? Or did nurses have medical licenses too? Why was he working as a receptionist?

Docta C’s pager buzzed, and he jumped to his feet, murmured, “Excuse me,” and strode out of the room.

“All right, I just need to get your chart updated,” said Renee, clicking into the computer in the corner of the room. As she added the first few notes to my chart, I quickly developed my line of questioning.

“I hope you don’t mind if I pry a little—why did Samuel lose his medical license?”

She crossed her arms and stared at me. “You’re asking a lot of questions.”

"It's not every day there's a murder in a hospital." I held her gaze.

She relented and went back to adding notes to the chart. "Listen," she said, "you really shouldn't worry. You need to just focus on your babies and on healing."

"Well, I can't see my babies right now, and I don't think meditating on my stitches is going to help them heal." I shrugged, trying to look nonchalant. "I was really into true crime and detective stories when I was pregnant."

It wasn't *technically* a lie. I'd *lived* a lot of true crime and detective stories during the pregnancy. And I didn't want to tip off Nurse Renee that I was an experienced private investigator—not when she was my prime suspect and I was in such a vulnerable state.

If she was the murderer, she wouldn't be threatened by a random mom with a true-crime addiction.

"So," I continued, "now there's a real true-crime story unfolding in front of us. Gives me something to think about, besides the fact that I"—my voice broke—"that I can't hold my babies yet."

I wasn't acting. Not really. It hurt that my babies were far away, getting poked and prodded and maybe even hooked up to tubes and wires. They should be here, in my arms, in the soft light of a delivery room.

"Besides!" I said, trying to sound bumbling and enthusiastic but still sympathetic—to get her to *want* to open up to me, whether she was guilty or not. "What if I think of something the police miss? You never know!"

Renee tapped a couple more keys, seeming to consider my words. "Well, I suppose it can't hurt. Samuel had his license to practice suspended three months ago. He used to be a NICU doctor."

I gasped. "What happened?"

"It *was* a DUI, actually," she said ruefully. "You were right about that. A DUI on the way home from work, no less."

"So, he was drunk while taking care of the NICU babies?" I asked, horrified.

"Honestly, I should have dumped him months earlier." She put the computer to sleep and sat in the chair next to my hospital bed. "He cheated on me at least three times, with three different women. But . . . I don't know. I thought he could change. Guess he won't change now."

I carefully studied her face. She looked resigned, but saddened.

She continued, "And I guess I had this picture of how my life was going to go. When I started out, I wasn't passionate being a nurse. I wanted to work for a few years and make decent money, then marry a doctor and be a stay-at-home mom when I started having my own babies. I almost broke up with Samuel the third time he cheated on me, because I'd begun to realize that I didn't need to marry a doctor—that I was happy in my nursing career. I've grown to love it. But I was afraid, I guess. Afraid I'd regret it."

I reached out and grabbed her hand. "That sounds so hard."

Tears brimmed in her eyes. "It was. When he got his license suspended, that was the last straw. He wasn't changing. He was still partying—and he'd escalated to drinking at work. He could have killed someone! And maybe he did."

That caught my attention. "Maybe he did? What does that mean?"

Could Samuel have given subpar care to the NICU infants? Would a grieving parent have returned to settle the score? *Now that's a motive.*

She shrugged. "I don't have any case in particular in mind. But NICU babies . . . it's not a hundred percent success rate."

Alarm flashed through me, and my eyes widened.

"Oh, no! Your babies will be fine!" she exclaimed. "They're really in the NICU as a precaution. I'm talking about the micro preemies, and a few of the extremely preterm babies . . . even with our best efforts, we can't save them all."

A haunted look shone in her eyes.

"So . . ." I said slowly, "you're saying that some babies died while Samuel was in charge?"

A tear trailed down her cheek, and she wiped it away with a sniffle. "I don't think we were losing more babies than normal, but . . . I don't know."

The implication nearly knocked me breathless. I thought of my precious, sweet sons in the NICU. Felt my love and devotion for them with the acutest intensity. I couldn't imagine what it would be like for one of my little ones to not make it.

Those poor parents . . .

The thought sent a tingle down my spine. *Definitely* a potential motive.

But that didn't mean Nurse Renee was in the clear. Police always scrutinized exes closely—and after such a recent breakup, when they still worked together, and she'd been so nearby when he was killed?

It was suspicious. I'd keep an eye on her.

But I didn't want her to *think* I was keeping an eye on her.

I started to lean forward—then glanced down at my bandaged stomach and thought better of it—and said, "Do you know if any of the grieving parents blamed Samuel for their baby's death?"

She sucked in a deep breath, and her hand flew to her mouth. "You don't think that—"

"Grief can make people do crazy things," I said sadly. "It wouldn't be the first time."

"I mean, he was killed here," she murmured. "Oh, goodness. That's so sad. Heaping tragedy on tragedy." She stood abruptly and shook her head. "But we don't know for sure that that was why." Her voice took on a darkly ironic tone. "Maybe it was one of the floozies he was sleeping with. He certainly . . . got around, shall we say. Maybe one of them found out about the others and—"

She stopped abruptly, whirled back around, and stared wide-eyed at me. "Oh, goodness. Do . . . do I need a lawyer? I'm an ex! And I was here in the hospital when it happened!"

I pressed my lips together, startled by the sudden shift. A sudden wave of exhaustion overtook me.

I just gave birth. To twins! Can I really do this? Take on a new case?

I didn't answer her question—I was playing a role of a wide-eyed young mom who liked true-crime documentaries, after all.

"I-I've got to call my boyfriend." She stood suddenly and bolted toward the door. "Hit the call button if you need anything. I'll be back to check on you in a few minutes."

Her boyfriend? That means she's already moved on.

I glanced from the door to the call button. "Well, this presents another problem," I muttered. "How am I supposed to investigate anything when I'm stuck in a room recovering from surgery?"

And even if I *could* leave the room, would I want to investigate? What I desperately wanted was time with my newborn sons. Time to meet them and cuddle them and pour fierce maternal love on them.

But . . . I swallowed back a wash of bile. *As awful a person as Samuel was, he was somebody's son.* Someone had given birth to him, had nursed him, had kissed his scraped knees and wept over his first broken heart.

Tears sprang to my eyes. *His poor mother. Does she know yet?*

I blinked away the tears, startled by the sudden well of emotion, picturing a woman, about sixty, aging gracefully, with features strikingly similar to Samuel's.

Must be the postpartum hormones.

But the picture wouldn't leave me, and a decision solidified deep in my gut.

I'll catch the person who did this, I promised.
There will be justice for your son.

CHAPTER TEN

I twiddled my thumbs and waited for someone to come check on me.

And waited.

And waited.

And waited.

I must have dozed off because I awoke to some commotion in the hallway. My ears pricked up.

The police must have arrived.

My fingers itched for my notebook and pen, to help organize my thoughts. But my purse was across the room, and I couldn't climb out of bed to get it in my current state.

Exhaustion gnawed at me, but the case wouldn't let me go.

"Okay," I whispered, "let's go over what we know."

I closed my eyes and pictured a legal-sized notepad, imagining scrawling out my notes.

Victim: Samuel Hall, late thirties.

Profession: NICU doctor, but with a temporary (at least? maybe permanently?) suspended license. Currently working as a receptionist in the maternity ward.

Hobbies: Drinking. Womanizing.

Suspects:

1. *Nurse Renee: ex-fiancée, was cheated on, broke up with him after his license was suspended. But apparently, already has a new boyfriend?*

2. *Nurse Bindi: thought he would burn in hell, for undetermined reasons.*
3. *Samuel's other lovers? Especially anyone who thought she was the only woman in his life.*
4. *The bereaved parents of Samuel's lost patients—especially anyone who knew about the DUI.*

"I need a pen and paper," I whispered. I reached for the call button, but before I pressed it, the door opened.

I glanced up, expecting Nurse Renee. But to my surprise and delight, my good friend Officer Deb stood in the doorway.

"Deb!" I cried out. "I'm so glad you're here."

She studied me skeptically. "You look exhausted."

I mustered a dry laugh. "I feel exhausted. I just had twins! And surgery."

"Your babies are doing great," she said. "I checked on that before I came in here. Figured you'd want to know."

A rush of gratitude flooded me. "Thank you." Tears sprang to my eyes again. "I hadn't realized how much I needed to hear that."

"And Jim is holding at least one of them at all times. They're getting plenty of love."

A soft smile sprang to my lips. "Thank you, Deb."

Then her expression turned serious. "You heard about the murder?"

I nodded. "I've already started compiling a list of suspects."

She chortled and closed the door behind her. "We all went back to the station after the party—figured we'd get a little more work done on that other case—and when we got the call about a murder in the maternity ward at the hospital, McNearny slammed the desk and yelled, 'Darn it, Connolly!'"

I chuckled and crossed my arms. "I might have been in a different hospital. He didn't know where I was giving birth."

"You have some kinda sixth sense for going where the murders happen," she said with a grin. "We figured we'd find you here. He'd have come in here himself to gripe at you, but I thought you might prefer to talk with a woman in your current state."

"Suppose that's another thing I should thank you for." I grinned. "At the very least, I prefer not to talk to *McNearny* in my current state. Let's wait until tomorrow for that at least."

"Well." She pulled up a chair to my bedside and whipped out a pen and paper. "You should probably let us handle most of the heavy lifting this time. You're in no condition to poke around and look for clues. Who's on your suspect list?"

I stared longingly at the pen, but Deb was right. If I wanted justice for Samuel, to bring some sense of closing and consolation to his poor mother, I had to accept my limitations and work more closely with the police on this case.

"I have four suspects so far," I said. "Well . . . two of them are *categories* of suspects."

I gave her the rundown on everything I'd learned from Nurse Renee—the cheating, the DUI, the breakup, the license suspension—plus the fight I'd overheard between Docta C and Nurse Bindi.

Deb gave a low whistle. "Sounds like a real piece of work."

"He was someone's son," I whispered, my voice suddenly husky.

She glanced up at me sharply, then her features relaxed. "Of course he was," she said. "And we'll bring the murderer to justice." She paused, then asked, "Do you have anything else for me?"

I shook my head. "Not yet."

"Need anything? Water? A snack?" She glanced at the monitors I was hooked up to and cracked a grin. "Morphine?"

Smirking, I said, "The epidural is still holding up. I'd like to see my babies, if you can pull any strings."

Deb nodded. "I'll pass the message along for you. Can you text me if you learn anything else?"

"Oh!" I pointed at my purse across the room. "Could you bring me my purse? My phone's in there."

As is a notepad and pen.

"Sure thing." She handed me my purse and headed for the door.

"Oh! Deb?"

She turned back around, one eyebrow raised. "Yeah?"

I grimaced. "Have you or McNearny told anyone I'm a private investigator?"

"Of course not," she said, as if the answer should be obvious. "There's a murderer on the loose, and you're not in any state to fight back if you're attacked. We don't need anyone offing the department's best private asset."

With a shaky smile, I said, "My thoughts exactly. I've been keeping it on the down-low, pretending that I'm asking questions because I like true-crime shows."

She laughed out loud. "That's a great cover story. You're one of a kind, Kate. Remember—text me if you find out anything. You can't be a lone cowgirl on this one."

"I promise."

She shook her head and muttered, "I can't believe you went into labor right before a murderer struck at your maternity ward. You really do have a sixth sense."

"A sixth sense? No, more like bad timing," I said.

"The worst," she agreed, opening the door and disappearing into the hall.

I riffled through the bag to find a pen and paper. It was a small notepad—the one I'd been using for my to-do list this month, not the legal-sized paper I preferred for cases—but it would do.

I jotted down my notes, observations, and suspicions, then tucked the notepad back in my purse so Nurse Renee wouldn't see it when she came back in.

Then I waited again.

The door opened, startling me awake.

I blinked, trying to reorient myself, and let out a huge yawn.

How long was I asleep? I still feel exhausted.

Nurse Renee entered the room, looking nearly as tired as I felt, her curly red hair pulled up into a messy bun.

She smiled at me, but it looked forced. "How's it going?" she asked.

"I still can't feel any pain," I said. "How are my babies?"

"They're doing great." Her tone reassured me. "It's just about the end of my shift, so I wanted to check on you and see if you needed anything."

"Can I see them?" I blurted.

She checked my surgery site and nodded. "I'll have an orderly come and take you to NICU."

Excitement flooded me. *If I could feel my feet, I'd tap dance on the bed!*

All thoughts of the case dropped away. I was going to see my babies!

Nurse Renee left, and I hummed a happy tune while I waited for the orderly. A few minutes later, the door opened again, and Mama Tina walked in, pushing a wheelchair.

"Well, hello again, my dear," she chirped. "I hear you're about to meet a couple of very special babies!"

She eased me into the wheelchair and pushed me down the hall. Three cops stood in a huddle in a doorway, including Deb and Sergeant McNearny. My eyes darted toward them as we passed by, but they didn't give any sign of recognition.

I set my jaw. This was like being undercover.

Deep undercover. I took a deep breath. "Police are still here?" I asked Mama Tina quietly. "I heard someone was killed."

Mama Tina let out a low whistle. "That poor front desk boy," she said. "Sad business."

"Does anyone know what happened yet?"

"Stabbed." She hesitated. "I mean, that's what I'm assuming. Caught a glimpse of the body before the cops arrived—there was definitely blood." She patted my shoulder. "But what am I talking about? You shouldn't have to think about such things on this happy day! Your babies are here!"

"I've just been thinking about the victim's mother," I said softly.

"Well," she said, her voice growing chipper again, "that's very sweet of you, and perfectly natural, I suppose. Yes, I'm sure this will bring grief to his mother—but that was already his habit, I think."

"What do you mean?" I asked, seizing the opening to corroborate Nurse Renee's story.

She tsked. "Let's just say Samuel had a history here at the hospital. He was very successful at his job, and he squandered it all."

"He was very successful as a receptionist?"

"Well, he used to have a different job. A better job."

"What happened? Did he get demoted too?"

She chuckled softly. "You could say that. Listen, I really shouldn't say more. The hospital doesn't want us to talk about it."

We crossed out of the maternity ward and into the NICU, passing another reception area and waiting room before heading down another hall. I let the conversation go, not wanting to ask too many questions where we might be overheard.

"And here we are!" exclaimed Mama Tina as we made the final turn.

I blinked, surprised and delighted at the sight. I'd expected a big, open room full of baby incubators, full of pacing, anxious parents and nurses moving from child to child.

But instead, I found myself in a private room with only two incubators. A tiny baby lay in one, hooked up to wires and tubes. Nurse Bindi was bent over him, adjusting one of the tubes. Next to the incubator, Jim sat holding the other baby, swaddled tightly in blankets.

"Jim!" I cried.

My husband looked up and gave me a huge smile. "Kate! I'm so glad you're here! Come meet the boys!"

He stood, and Mama Tina wheeled me over to him. My breath caught in my throat as Jim handed me the baby.

"He's perfect!" I whispered, feeling his sweet little warmth against me.

I glanced at the baby in the incubator, feeling suddenly sad. "What's wrong?" I asked. "Is he all right?"

"He's just fine!" Nurse Bindi said, her head popping up. "Just a little small, which is to be expected in twins born early, and we're helping him work on his breathing a little bit."

"His breathing?" Panic flooded me.

Bindi clasped her hands together. "Don't you worry about a thing, mama. We'll have him out of here in no time at all. Two or three days at the most. He's not in any danger, and he'll get the best care I can give him. I'd do anything for my little NICU angels!"

I kissed my son's soft forehead, and Jim moved over to sit next to the incubator, resting his hand on the other's baby's tummy.

"Have you been here all night?" I asked Jim.

He nodded. "Mom was here for a long time too, but I sent her home to rest."

"What should we name them?" I asked, marveling at their perfect, miniature features. "I've . . . been thinking of names for girls!"

"Me too," said Jim. "What about . . . Lawrence and Lucas?"

I wrinkled my nose. "We can't have a Laurie and a Lawrence. I do like Lucas, though. What about Logan and Lucas?"

Jim tilted his head and stared down at the baby in the incubator. "I don't feel like Logan fits either of them, to tell you the truth."

"Well, the names don't need to start with *L*, do they?"

We tossed names back and forth for about ten minutes, and then I laughed aloud. "Well, we don't have to name them right away. Let's give them nicknames for now, and we can keep thinking about it."

"Thing One and Thing Two?" asked Jim. "Like in Dr. Seuss?"

"Oh no!" I crooned, reaching down to caress the baby's nose. "We can't possible call such perfect little angels *things*."

"Hmm," said Jim, his eyes sparkling. "Well, how Tweedledee and Tweedledum."

I tried to purse my lips in disapproval, but I couldn't suppress the giggle that squeaked out of me. "Not that, either. Can we find something a little more dignified?"

He tilted his head. "How about Primus and Secundus?"

My forehead wrinkled. "What and what?"

"Primus and Secundus. It means *first* and *second* in Latin. The film I'm about to start doing marketing design for is a period piece set in Ancient Rome, and the main character is a second-born son named Secundus."

I cracked a smile. "I like that. As the placeholder nickname. Not their real names, of course."

"Might work for real names . . ." Jim mused.

"Not a chance." I kissed the baby's forehead. "But we'll call them that until we come up with something we both like."

"Well, you're holding Primus over there," said Jim. "He was born first."

"Hello, sweet Primus," I cooed. "I'm your mama, and I missed you so much."

I'm not sure how long I sat there holding Primus, marveling at the miracle of motherhood, at how much I loved these new babies so dearly already.

But my mood immediately soured when Docta C entered the room. "There you are," he snapped. "I've been looking for you. I didn't sign off on you moving to the NICU. You need to be sleeping. We're going to have you up and walking around in a few hours."

Nurse Bindi stalked in behind him and crossed her arms. "Dr. Phillips," she said in a clipped tone, "perhaps you'd like to be a little more compassionate with this new mama here."

He let out a sigh and raked a hand through his hair. "Sorry," he murmured to me. "It's just been quite a day, and I got worried when I couldn't find you. There's a murderer on the loose, after all."

"And what makes you think any of our moms and babies would be in danger?" she snapped. "And even if you did, what gives you the right to scare her like that?"

Jim and I shared a long, wide-eyed glance.

What's going on with this place? I'd never seen so much open animosity in any professional setting—much less in a healthcare facility.

And in the maternity ward and NICU, no less.

Docta C's jaw dropped as if he, too, was surprised at how much Bindi had let her guard down in front of a patient. "I . . . I just—"

She shoved past him. "No one who killed Samuel Hall is going to go after the moms and babies here. If anything, the killer did them a favor. They made sure Samuel will never practice medicine again."

My mind raced as I took in the fierce expression on her face. She didn't look at all sad or shocked about Samuel's murder.

In fact, the expression in her eyes sent chills down my spine.

If I didn't know any better, I'd think she was happy he's dead.

CHAPTER ELEVEN

My mind raced as I lay in my hospital bed in the recovery room, trying to sleep. Acute loneliness flooded me, but I resisted the urge to text Jim to ask him to come give me a hug.

I'd told Jim to stay with the babies. I couldn't be with them, so he needed to be. I wanted them to have a parent at their side at all times, to not be alone in a hospital on their first full day in the outside world.

We really should name them.

They could only be Primus and Secundus so long—names like that would get them bullied in kindergarten.

We can't let Mom know that those are the nicknames we've given them. She'll think they're perfectly offbeat and charming and try to browbeat us into keeping them.

Aidan and Caidyn? Jason and Jeremy? Jim Jr and . . . Archibald?

I let out a heavy sigh. My suggestions were starting to sound like Jim's.

The first hints of daylight crept through the curtains, and I still hadn't fallen asleep. My mind wandered back to that strange interaction with Nurse Bindi.

She clearly loathed Samuel.

Did she blame him for the deaths of any NICU babies? Bindi herself had said she'd do anything for her *little NICU angels*.

Did *anything* include murder?

"But Samuel's license had been suspended," I murmured. "There weren't any babies in danger."

Maybe the licensing board was going to give him his license back? I made a mental note to ask Deb to look into that angle.

All at once, afternoon sunlight streamed into my room and Nurse Renee was standing at my bedside. I blinked up at her, disoriented.

I must have fallen asleep after all.

"Morning, new mama!" she said. "It's time for your next round of pain medicine, and the doctor wants you to try walking around. Do you think you're up for that?"

I yawned, grimacing when I realized how much my C-section wound hurt. "Yeah, I think I'm going to need that medicine."

She handed me a pill and a small cup of water.

I swallowed it back and squinted at her. "You're back already?"

She nodded, soft sadness shining in her eyes. "The nurse who found the body had a panic attack and asked to take today off. They moved a few shifts around as a result, and I agreed to come in early. I think work will help take my mind off of . . . well, everything."

"Did you sleep all right?" I asked.

"Well enough to do my job," she said. "And that's all that matters."

She slowly helped me to my feet, and I let out a sharp gasp. "Ooooh."

"Is that too much?" She eased me back down.

I bit my lip. "It hurt, but I think I was it was more dizzying than painful. Do you think I could get some food before we try again?"

"Yeah, I'll have some sent up." She paused. "Did . . . did you ever hear exactly what happened to Samuel? I know you were trying to play sleuth."

I shook my head, my thoughts lighting up with suspicion. No way was I giving information to a potential suspect. The less she thought I knew, the more likely she was to incriminate herself.

"No . . . I think I kinda forgot about all that after you left, to be honest. I just keep thinking about how much I miss my babies."

She chewed her lip, looking disappointed. "I'll have that food sent up, and I'll be back in a while."

A few minutes later, another staff member delivered me a plate of hospital food—a slice of unappetizing-looking chicken and a side of lukewarm peas that must have come straight out of a can.

Not exactly gourmet, but I'll take what I can get. I was so hungry that it didn't taste half bad.

After another hour, Nurse Renee returned. "Should we try this again?" she asked with a soft but strained smile.

"Sure! I think I'll be a little steadier this time." I tried to act natural, like I didn't suspect her of murder.

She helped me to my feet, and this time, I was able to stand unassisted.

"I'm definitely sore," I said, "but it's a lot easier to stand. Can I see my babies again?"

"We'll get you over there again soon." She chuckled. "But the doctor wants to make sure you're moving again. Recovery after a C-section can be tough."

I took a few steps, then lurched forward, nearly running into the wall. "It's like I'm still pregnant," I grumbled, turning back around and leaning against the wall. "I'm so bloated."

With a sympathetic shrug, Renee said, "Yeah, those IV liquids are bloating. So, did the cops ever interview you about Samuel?"

Surprised by the quick change in subjects, I stuttered, "Uh . . . no?"

She looked confused, and I struggled to clarify.

"I mean, yeah, a policewoman did come talk to me, but I wouldn't call it an *interview*, exactly. I think she just wanted to know if I'd seen anything out of the ordinary, but I couldn't tell her much of anything . . . since I was giving birth when the murder happened."

"They interviewed me," she blurted. "It was the woman. Detective Fisher. Must have been the same one who interviewed you."

"Oh," I said lightly. "How'd that go?" I lowered my voice to a conspiratorial whisper. "Did you find out anything interesting?"

But Renee just seemed distressed. "She was asking me all sorts of questions about my breakup with Samuel. It was like she thought I was a suspect! But I know I'm not—I could never be . . ."

My lips twitched. "But the police don't know that yet. They have to overturn every clue, and murders are often committed by a significant other or an ex. At least that's what the true-crime documentaries and detective novels say."

"But they should know I'd never do it," she said weakly.

I raised an eyebrow. "What do you mean?"

"I . . . never mind. I just can't believe . . ."

Another thing that seemed suspicious about Renee, I noted. She was either hiding something, or she was entitled—like she thought she was too special for the police to even *consider* her as a suspect . . . when her ex had been murdered!

Could she be a narcissist? If she was the killer, narcissism might explain how she struck in cold blood and went back to work immediately afterward without any apparent remorse.

Something was off about Renee. I just wasn't sure what.

"Well," I said, taking a few steps back toward the bed. "All you have to do is prove your alibi, right? Prove that you were somewhere else when the murder happened?"

"That's just the problem," she whispered. "I can't. I told that policewoman to just check the tapes. We have cameras in all the halls, for security reasons. But she said there's something wrong with the tapes and they can't see any of them."

Something wrong with the tapes? *That means it was an inside job. Someone tampered with the cameras in advance.*

That probably ruled out any grieving parents, and it *certainly* made the hospital staff a whole lot more suspicious.

"And I . . . I left the delivery room for a few minutes. It took me a little while to find an orderly, and that was right in the window when Samuel was—"

Her voice cracked. "When Samuel was killed."

I sank back down to sit on the bed and reached out to grab her hand. "It's going to be all right," I said firmly. "They'll bring the real killer to justice. I'm sure of it."

I watched her face closely for any flicker of reaction, but I couldn't read her. Couldn't tell whether she was comforted or terrified by my words.

She abruptly changed the subject, and I didn't pry further while she helped me practice walking. I didn't want to raise her suspicions—I still hoped to get more information out of her, and I was still vulnerable in her care.

"All right," she finally said. "The doctor wants you to walk around for an hour or two, and then we'll see about getting you back for another visit with the babies."

I certainly wasn't going to argue with that! I'd cooperate with anything that would earn me another visit with my sweet little angels.

So I walked the halls, feeling absolutely, positively like a bloated walrus. I glanced down at the hospital gown I was wearing, feeling a sense of panic. Had I been this bloated after giving birth to Laurie? Was this normal? Or was I doomed to look and feel like a pregnant lady forever?

I hadn't lost my Laurie-pregnancy weight before getting pregnant with the twins. Would that make a difference?

This is the least of my concerns, I chided myself. *The babies are being taken care of, and we're all going to go home soon, and that's what matters.*

Besides, I knew I was being silly. I was just bloated. I *would* lose the baby weight eventually, if I didn't have another surprise pregnancy.

Right?

Focus on something else. Murderers. We've got to find a murderer.

I walked around the corner and nearly collided with none other than Sergeant McNearny.

CHAPTER TWELVE

"K-kate?" Sergeant McNearny stammered, blanching.

My eyebrows knit together, and I squinted at him. "McNearny? What are you doing here?" I studied him. "And with . . . flowers?"

The officer was carrying a bouquet of fresh flowers in a small vase—red roses, no less!

His mouth opened, then closed. Finally, he held them out and blurted, "They're-they're for you."

I tried—and failed—to suppress a snort. "You . . . brought me a bouquet of red roses?"

"S-seemed like the new mom should have some flowers. The grocery store had roses. I can take them back . . ."

"No." I reached out and accepted the offering. "They're perfectly lovely. I'm just surprised. I'll set them up in my room."

Of course Sergeant McNearny is clueless that red roses are usually a romantic offering. Men.

But I'd accept the gift with gratitude, in the spirit it was intended. It was actually a very sweet gesture on his part.

We butted heads on cases all the time, but over the last year, we'd moved from cold antipathy to grudging respect to the beginning of something like friendship.

I nodded down the hall. "My room is just back there. I'll put the flowers where I can appreciate them."

We headed toward the room, my steps slow and tight.

Will I ever walk normally again?

I turned to McNearny and said in a low voice, "So, what can you tell me about the case?"

McNearny snorted. "Not much. I've decided to let Fisher take the lead on this one."

"Deb?"

That surprised me even more than the display of red roses. Deb had earned a promotion a little while back, and she'd worked enough murder cases to qualify her to head one up . . . but McNearny didn't relinquish control lightly.

"Yeah. Thought it was time to let her stretch her wings."

We reached the doorway to my room just as a warm, familiar voice called, "Kate!"

I turned, and a huge smile lit up my face. My husband was walking down the hall toward me.

"Jim!" I cried. "How are the babies?"

"They're doing great! Oh, hey, McNearny!" He stopped and stared at the flowers in my hand. "Oh, who sent flowers?"

I smirked. "McNearny brought them. Wasn't that sweet of him?"

Jim elbowed McNearny in the ribs. "Wouldn't have thought you were the sentimental type. That's actually really nice."

McNearny muttered under his breath, "Well, I'll certainly never make that mistake again."

With a laugh, Jim said, "Hey, some niceness looks good on you."

McNearny shifted his weight from foot to foot. "Well, I had to come here anyway to check on the case."

Why is he acting so strangely?

Jim leaned forward and gently kissed my forehead. "I just came by to check on you, honey. How are you feeling?"

I leaned up against him. "Definitely sore, and definitely missing my babies, but good otherwise."

"It's so good to see you up and walking around. The twins are doing great. The nurse said they should be able to go home in just a couple days."

"Oh, that's wonderful," I said, breathing out some of the tension I'd been holding. Standing there with my head on my husband's shoulder, I soaked in his love and care, letting it warm the loneliness that had settled in on me overnight.

But then I stepped back. "Thank you for coming to see me. But . . . go back to them now, all right? I can't stand the thought of one of us not being there with them."

"Of course," he said, beaming at me. "I'm so glad you're doing better. Do you want to come see them?"

"Yes!" I exclaimed.

But just then Docta C strode around the corner, and all my hopes of sneaking out for a visit popped like a bubble.

"All right, Mrs. Connolly," he called, "let's get you back into the room so I can check on how you're doing."

My shoulder slumped, but Jim tilted my chin up.

"We'll sneak you out there later," he whispered.

"I heard that," Docta C said, his tone unamused. "We'll make sure she gets a visit with the twins as soon as we have the staff to manage it, but she can't leave the maternity wing on foot. We'll need to have an orderly take her over there in a wheelchair."

My hands balled into fists, and I was seized with the unaccountable urge to smack Docta C in the jaw. If I could walk here, why not in the NICU?

I dug my fingernails into my palms to keep from committing assault in front of a police officer.

Just new mom hormones. I inhaled deeply and exhaled. *Just new mom hormones.*

I didn't usually have fantasies of violence, but I was getting pretty darn fed up with this arrogant doctor . . . and pretty desperate to hold my babies.

The boys are safe and cared for, I reminded myself. *They're not in any danger. You don't have to fight for them.*

So I bit my lip and nodded at Docta C.

"Hey!" Jim slapped McNearny on the back. "Want to come meet the twins? They're boys!"

McNearny squinted, confused. "Didn't you guys *just* announce you were having two girls?"

"We were wrong! Come on!"

Jim and McNearny headed down the hall, and I stared after them, forlorn.

Why does McNearny get to see the babies, and I can't? I'm their mother!

But I begrudgingly cooperated as Docta C escorted me back into my hospital room. I set the flowers on the counter where I had a good view of them and sank down onto the bed as Docta C ran through a few questions with me.

"Listen," he said. "I need you to focus on rest and recovery. Unscheduled C-section are harder on new moms, because you've done both parts now the labor and the surgery. Ok? I need you to promise me you're going to rest."

"I will," I lied.

But by the time he left, I was starting to feel a sleepy again. *Must be the pain medicine kicking in,* I thought groggily. I let my eyelashes flutter closed and welcomed the sleep.

Sleep would get me an hour or two closer to going home with my babies.

"Daaaaaarling!"

My mother's voice interrupted my slumber. I blinked, vaguely disoriented. Mom and Galigani were at my bedside . . . and Mom was carrying Laurie!

I could have cried with joy. "Laurie!" I exclaimed, reaching for my baby girl. "Happy birthday, little duck!"

Laurie reached back, and I motioned for Mom to set her on my left side, so she wouldn't jostle the C-section wound.

I hugged her close, relieved to have *one* of my babies in my arms.

Then my jaw dropped. "Her hair!" I wailed.

Laurie's beautiful curls had been chopped off until she was nearly bald!

Bald was an overstatement, maybe, but whatever haircut my mom had given her had been an absolute butcher job, leaving Laurie's hair hacked in uneven tufts above the ear.

Mom, apparently mistaking my horror for joy, grinned and nudged Galigani. "We brought a present!"

Only then did I notice the absolutely massive gift bag that Galigani was carrying. He shot me an apologetic grimace as he handed it to me.

In sheer disbelief, I reached into the bag and pulled out a twenty-by-thirty-inch collage picture frame. In the center, two compartments were labeled *Baby's First Curl* and *Baby's First Tooth*. In the *Baby's First Curl* compartment, a long lock of Laurie's perfect hair lay limp and lifeless.

The rest of the collage was half-filled with photos of Laurie—the largest of them showing a grinning, shorn Laurie in a photo studio, clutching the most hideous of stuffed animals.

Is that a stuffed . . . fish?

"I thought about what you were saying about wanting Laurie's first birthday to be special, and since you couldn't be there, I decided we'd have an incredible girls' day full of memories."

Memories? Laurie's a year old! What memories will she have?

"She . . . won't remember it?" I offered weakly.

"That's why we documented it! So she'll have the pictures forever! I took her to the mall, and we got a haircut"—she ticked off numbers on her fingers—"and then to the aquarium, where I bought her a darling stuffed eel! She really seemed interested in the eels."

Ah. I glanced back at the picture. It was an eel, not a stuffed fish.

Mom continued, "Then we went back to the mall for a special birthday outfit and a photoshoot! Oh, and I booked that family photo session you wanted while we were there. In fact, I really should thank *you* for asking me to do that! That was what inspired me to take her for a beauty day and a first-birthday photoshoot!"

I looked more closely at the photo and bit back another gasp. Laurie was wearing an absolute monstrosity of an outfit—a sparkly, multicolored dress absolutely covered in ruffles and long fringe. The dress somehow simultaneously evoked a disco party, a flapper dress, and the Victorian era.

I glanced down at Laurie, who was resting her head against my chest. She was currently wearing one of the many *respectable* dresses I'd bought for her.

A small mercy.

"Oh, and you changed her out of the birthday dress already," I murmured.

"Well, I also got her an ice cream, and she drooled chocolate all over it," Mom said. "But the dry cleaner assured me that the dress will be as good as new by the time we get it back!"

"I hope not," I muttered.

"Hmm?" Mom warbled, her tone still perfectly self-satisfied.

"Nothing! Well . . ." I searched for some suitable response, sharing a long look with Galigani.

He shrugged helplessly and said, "I wasn't on the girls' day. She brought Laurie home and told me about all the . . . fun things they did."

In other words, don't blame me!

I let out a slow, frustrated breath. "Well, this is a lot of surprises! And it is *so good* to see my little duck!"

After a pause, Galigani said, "Vera told me there was a murder here last night."

I kissed the top of Laurie's head and sighed. "Yes, the receptionist was killed while I was in labor, I'm afraid."

"You're not on the case, are you?" Mom crossed her arms. "In your condition?"

My nose twitched. "I wouldn't say I'm on the case, *exactly*. My friend Deb Fisher is leading the investigation, and I haven't told anyone that I'm a private investigator, for my own safety."

"Good call," Galigani replied, rubbing the back of his neck. "You don't want that information getting out. Especially if the murderer is a hospital employee."

"My thoughts exactly." I snuggled Laurie closer. "I'm just asking people a few questions here and there, gathering information, reporting back to Deb."

Mom threw her arms in the air. "You call that *not* being on the case?"

"Well, no one's hired me," I said, knowing how weak my protests sounded. "And I'm not exactly conducting a full-on investigation and formally interviewing people. I'm just trying to see if I can uncover any leads. I promise I'll let Deb handle the rest."

"Hmm," said Galigani. "Who was the victim? I'll run him through the PI database and see if I can come up with anything useful."

"His name was Samuel Hall," I said. I quickly gave them the rundown of everything I'd heard about Samuel—though I left off the suspicious conversation I'd overheard between Nurse Bindi and Docta C. I didn't want to worry my mom about the babies' safety.

"Your nurse is his ex?" Mom screeched. "You need a new nurse! Why is she even still working here?"

Galigani patted her shoulder. "There, there, Vera. Sounds like this Samuel guy made a lot of enemies. No reason to think that this particular ex is the top suspect."

"But," I said slowly, "you might want to look into her, too. She's behaving a little suspiciously, and I do have some questions about her."

"Right-o." Galigani nodded. "I'll let you know what I find."

Just then, Mama Tina pushed a wheelchair into the room. "Why, hello again!" she chirped.

I smiled at her, but worry churned in my gut. Had she overheard any of our conversation? If so, was she close to Nurse Renee? Would she tell anyone that I was a private investigator?

But if Mama Tina had heard us talking, she gave no indication of it.

"Ready to see those babies again?" she asked.

CHAPTER THIRTEEN

After I returned from my visit to the NICU, I got a phone call from Galigani.

"Hey kid," he said. "Found some weird stuff on that Samuel Hall guy."

"Oh?" I sat up a little straighter and rubbed my eyes. "What kind of weird stuff?"

"He got demoted like four months ago, right?"

"Right . . ."

"Get this—he still rents a really ritzy apartment downtown, and he just renewed the lease on it last week!"

I tilted my head. "How could he afford that?"

"My thoughts exactly. And I've found his social media accounts—seems like he partied a lot at expensive nightclubs."

"Maybe he'd saved a lot of money? Or had a trust fund or something."

"Could be," Galigani mused, "but does he sound like the kind of guy who stockpiles his money carefully?"

"Did you find out anything about Renee?"

"She was arrested once for a domestic dispute—sounds like she threw a knife at her roommate, but no charges were ever filed."

I gasped aloud. "And Samuel was stabbed!"

"That's an awfully big coincidence. Sure makes that nurse seem more suspicious."

There was a knock on my doorframe, and I looked up to see Paula standing there.

"Hey, Galigani," I said, "I've got to go—Paula's here. But thanks for the update. Keep me posted if you come across anything else." I hung up the phone and grinned at Paula. "Well, hello there! It's good to see your face!"

"I'm so sorry you had to have that C-section!" exclaimed Paula. "And now the babies are stuck in the NICU!"

"It's been a crazy twenty-four hours." I ran a hand through my hair. "Did you hear there was a murder?"

She gasped aloud. "No! Here? At the hospital? Is that why you were talking to Galigani?"

"Close the door, and I'll tell you all about it."

Paula shut the door behind her, and I spilled the whole story to her. When I described what Galigani had learned, she looked genuinely frightened.

"Kate! If you think your nurse is a killer, you've got to tell Deb. You can't stay here with a killer taking care of you!"

"It's fine, Paula. The nurse doesn't have any reason to think I'm suspicious of her. And I'm going to tell Deb everything, I promise. I've only *just* gotten off the phone with Galigani."

Paula crossed her arms. "You text Deb right now. I don't trust you not to lone-ranger this, even when you're in the hospital."

"Fiiiiiiine," I chuckled as I typed out a text to Deb. "That's probably fair. I've earned those suspicions."

When I'd sent Deb the update, I looked up to see Paula smelling the roses.

"Oh, these are just lovely!" she exclaimed. "Jim is so sweet."

"They're not from Jim," I said with a smirk.

"Oh?" She arched an elegant eyebrow. "You have a secret admirer, then? Why would anyone else send red roses?"

I laughed out loud. "I certainly *hope* he's not an admirer. McNearny brought the flowers to me this afternoon."

Paula's jaw dropped. "*McNearny* brought you these flowers?"

I nodded.

She crossed her arms and leaned back against the counter, studying me skeptically. "McNearny brought you *red roses*?"

Cracking my neck, I said, "He doesn't mean anything by it. It seemed like a sweet gesture, if a little weird."

Paula whirled back around and studied the flowers. "Hey!" she exclaimed. "There's a note in here!"

"What?" I wrinkled my nose. "Why would he include a note? He brought the flowers in person."

Paula snatched a slip of paper from the depths of the roses and held it aloft. Then she read it quietly to herself . . . and shrieked out loud.

"What?" I demanded, my mind racing. "What does it say?"

My best friend stared at me, her lips pursed. "Well, either McNearny is in love with you—"

I burst out laughing, then stopped abruptly when I realized she was serious.

"—or," she continued, "these flowers weren't meant for you."

Had he bought the roses for a girlfriend? Two or three months ago, McNearny had said he was seeing someone, but I'd never learned who his girlfriend was.

I stared at the flowers. They *were* red roses. Maybe McNearny wasn't so clueless after all.

But wouldn't that mean his girlfriend worked here at the hospital? Had I accidentally intercepted him when he was bringing her flowers?

Because if there were two things I was absolutely certain of in this life, it was this: I would die for any of my children, and Sergeant Patrick McNearny wasn't in love with me.

"What does the note say?" I demanded.

Paula took a deep breath and read aloud. "My dearest, I'm so sorry you're having such a dreadful day. Remember that I'm always here for you. Love, Pat."

I stared at Paula.

She stared back at me.

I stared back at her.

"Well," I said after a long silence, "those flowers certainly *weren't* meant for me."

"Why would he have given them to you, then?" She crossed her arms.

The realization hit me. "Because he panicked," I said slowly. "He didn't expect to run into me, and he didn't want to tell me that his girlfriend works here at the hospital."

She crossed over to the chair at my bedside. "But why would he hide that? He's been divorced since before you even met him. Had he told you he *wasn't* seeing anyone?"

"No, he'd mentioned a girlfriend to me offhandedly . . ."

She sat down and rested her chin on her hands. "This doesn't make any sense at all!"

One piece of the puzzle clicked into place.

"I think it does!" I snatched my small notepad out of my purse and began scribbling notes to organize my thoughts. "He also said he was letting Deb take the lead on this investigation!"

She wrinkled her nose. "He is? Last time I went out with Deb, she was complaining that he always babysat the detectives and wasn't letting her handle cases."

I snapped my fingers. "So, there's a reason he's suddenly giving up control to Deb."

"A conflict of interest!" She sucked in a sharp gasp. "He knows he's too close to this case."

"So, who's the woman?" I murmured. "She must work in the maternity ward, or I wouldn't have run into him."

A new suspicion itched at the corner of my mind. *What if . . . ?*

"Could it be my nurse?" I asked. "Renee? She said she has a boyfriend, and . . . she left to call her boyfriend right after the murder!"

Paula's eyes popped wide. "No! It couldn't be . . . could it?"

I set my pen down. "I'm probably letting my imagination run away with me, but . . ."

"Well . . . what are you going to do about that? Should you tell Deb?"

My lips twitched. "What am I supposed to tell her? That he can't be objective? I've solved a lot of cases where people told me I couldn't be objective."

Paula winced—I'd struck close to home. Not too long ago, Paula herself had been a murder suspect. I'd cleared her and put the real killer behind bars.

"That's fair," she said, her voice quavering a little. "But . . . what if his girlfriend really is a killer, and he just doesn't know it?"

"Hmm." My eyes lit up. "I have an idea!"

I pulled my phone back out and typed out a text message to McNearny: *Are you dating Renee??*

Before I hit *send*, I showed it to Paula.

"What are you doing?" she exclaimed. "You don't want him to know that we know!"

"But we *don't* know yet," I pointed out. "We just know that his girlfriend works here. If our suspicions are correct, I bet we'll get a visit from McNearny himself in the next hour or two."

Slowly and painfully, I pushed myself to a standing position.

"Where are you going? Shouldn't you be resting?" Paula asked.

I grinned at her. "I've been resting. Help me walk the halls for a little while. My mind is spinning on the case, and I want to see if we can glean any more information before McNearny gets here."

Paula and I walked up and down the halls for about five minutes. I tried to pull another nurse into conversation, but she apologized and said she didn't have time for chitchat—she had too many patients to check on. She looked . . . frightened.

That's odd.

But maybe I was imagining her fear. She was probably just harried and overworked. Weren't hospitals chronically short-staffed?

"That's the problem with solving a murder in a hospital," I groused to Paula under my breath. "Everyone's too busy to cajole for information. If only I had a badge."

"Just tell Deb what you're thinking and let her finish the investigation," she whispered. "*She* has a badge!"

"I *am* telling Deb what I'm thinking," I retorted. "I'm just . . . trying to find out more."

Just then, Mama Tina pushed an empty wheelchair around the corner.

"Well, hello there, Miss Kate," she said cheerily. "It's good to see you up and around again. How are you feeling?"

Mama Tina! Now *there* was someone I could try to get information out of.

"Connolly!" barked a stern voice.

I turned, surprised to see McNearny striding down the hall. *Already?*

"That was fast," Paula whispered.

"Too fast," I replied.

"I'm sorry, I think I have to go speak with this gentleman," I said to Mama Tina. "But I'd love to talk to you later."

"I'm just going to take this wheelchair down to a patient," she said sweetly. "I'm glad you're feeling better."

She wheeled away, and McNearny ground to a halt in front of me.

"I need to talk to you," he said tersely. "In private."

I glanced at Paula, then back at McNearny.

He rolled his eyes. "She can come, I guess. I don't care. But we need to be away from any . . . listening ears."

"We can go back to my room," I said. "It's just three doors down."

Paula linked arms with me, and I hobbled behind McNearny, whose steps seemed animated with frenetic energy.

Three more officers appeared at the end of the hall, and Paula and I shared a long look.

We entered my room, and McNearny slammed the door behind us.

"You're a darn good PI, Connolly," he began. "And it doesn't even pain me to say it anymore. I need your help."

"Was I right?" I asked, crossing my arms.

"Of course you were." He ran a hand through his hair. "I never should have given you those stupid flowers with that note inside them. Yes! I'm seeing Renee!"

I chewed my lip. "How old is she?"

"We have a little bit of an age gap, but she doesn't care about that. She asked *me* out—I wasn't out chasing younger women." He threw his arms out. "And we have a problem."

"What problem is that?" *That you suspect your much-younger girlfriend is a killer?*

He paced the room once, twice, three times, then stopped abruptly and pivoted toward me. "There's been another murder."

CHAPTER FOURTEEN

Another murder?

Paula squeaked in fright.

I studied McNearny, taking in the raw fear in his eyes, the coiled energy in his muscles. He was a complete wreck.

"Sit down," I said gently. "Tell me what happened."

We sat across from each other, him on the chair and me on the hospital bed. Paula hovered near the door.

"We just got a call," he said through gritted teeth. "A doctor was killed. Stabbed just like Samuel Hall."

I tried to corral my racing thoughts. The stupid pain medication was making me feel dull and sluggish. "An OBGYN? Who?"

"Cory Phillips."

I clapped a hand over my mouth to dull my involuntary shriek. "Docta C's dead?" I hissed.

"Oh!" He sat up, as if startled. "He was your doctor?"

"Uh . . . I . . . temporarily, I guess," I stammered. "My regular OBGYN is on her way back from Rome. Dr. Phillips delivered the twins."

McNearny clenched his hands and leaned forward, staring straight down at the floor. "I'm sorry. Yes, he's been murdered. Here at the hospital."

I sucked in a sharp breath. "That's not good."

I hadn't liked the man as a person or a doctor, but I was sorry he was dead.

That argument with Nurse Bindi replayed in my mind.

She hated both Samuel and Docta C. *Looks like we have a new prime suspect.*

"And this brings me to my problem," McNearny continued. "Renee . . . used to be engaged to Samuel Hall, and she had a history with Cory Phillips as well."

My gaze snapped to him. *Renee had a what?*

Maybe Bindi wasn't the top suspect after all.

"What kind of history?" I asked slowly. "They dated?"

"They weren't a couple or anything." He hissed through his teeth. "They went on a few dates. Then Dr. Phillips told her that he wanted to continue to see her, but he wanted the freedom to see other people as well. Renee told him that was selfish, and they were on bad terms for a while. This was before she even started dating Samuel."

"I see."

He continued, his voice anguished. "I know what it looks like. Two men dead at the hospital she works at, while she was on duty. Stabbed so that they'd bleed out quickly—which means the killer either did their research or had some medical knowledge. And she had histories with both of them."

I rested my hands on the bed and leaned back. "You're right—that doesn't look great."

"But I know she didn't do it."

"How?"

He jerked upward and met my gaze. "Because I *know* her. And I know murder cases. She's a flawed human being, but she's not a killer."

I bit my lip.

"Connolly." He folded his hands in his lap. "We've been here before, but it was you assuring me that you knew someone wasn't a killer." He nodded at Paula. "She was one of them."

"I know," I whispered.

"And I couldn't take your word for it at the time, so I don't expect you to take mine. But I need your help. I need your powers of observation, your skill at putting information together. If you follow the evidence to its conclusion, I know you're going to figure out that it wasn't Renee."

My forehead creased. "Are you trying to hire me?"

"Yes."

"Are *you* trying to hire me, as a private citizen, or is the *department* trying to hire me?"

He winced at the question. "I . . . don't know. When you phrase it like that, it sounds like an ethics investigation waiting to happen, doesn't it? If I hire you as a private citizen, then I really have to recuse myself from the case, not just from being the lead investigator. If I hire you through the department . . . well, I obviously can't do that in this situation."

"Plus, I'm on maternity leave," I deadpanned, raising a skeptical eyebrow.

"Yeah, but you're living at the crime scene. You have to be here anyway. And we both know you'll be poking around."

The desperation in his eyes tugged at my heart. I knew that sense of desperation, that sinking feeling that someone I loved was being framed for murder.

"Does Deb know about Renee?" I asked.

He hissed through his teeth. "No."

"All right." I crossed my arms. "Here's how this is going to go. You need to tell Deb about your connection to the case, and officially recuse yourself from it. Then, you and I can work together on our own time, alongside the police investigation. That will keep you from getting in trouble or jeopardizing the official investigation, and I'm sure that, between the two of us, we can figure out who did this and clear Renee's name."

If she is, in fact, innocent. And if she's not, I'm going to have to break McNearny's heart.

ABOUT AN HOUR LATER, my phone buzzed with a text message from Deb, jolting me from a half sleep. *Can I come talk to you?*

All clear, I replied, yawning and trying to shake the cobwebs out of my brain. *No one here but me.*

Fifteen minutes later, she opened the door, and I sat up, finally wide awake.

"Hey," she said, pointing up at the clock, which read 9:59 and fifty seconds. "I'm just about off my shift. Promised myself I'd quit at ten if there weren't any urgent leads to follow. And at this point . . . there are not."

"Four, three, two, one!" I cried, counting down the seconds.

She dramatically reached into her jacket pocket and pulled out a flask of liquor.

"Deb!" I crossed my arms.

"What?" She grinned. "I waited until I was off-duty."

"I worry about you sometimes, you know that?"

She shrugged off my concern and took a swig. "Wanted to come talk to you about the case, and I preferred to do it after I'd clocked out. Had an interesting conversation with Sergeant McNearny this evening."

"What'd he tell you?"

I didn't want to betray McNearny's confidence, but I also wanted to make sure he'd told Deb the truth . . . or at least enough of it.

"That he's been dating my top suspect for like four months! I wanted to slap him upside the head! Anyway, I know he's my boss, but he made *me* the lead detective on this case, and I asked him to keep himself off it."

She took another swig from the flask, then tucked it back into her pocket. "It's one thing for a PI to be too close to a suspect. It's entirely another for a police officer to be. That could open up all kinds of accusations, get evidence thrown out in court . . . even if he's right, and his girlfriend is innocent, that sort of conflict of interest could mean our real killer gets off on a technicality."

I nodded solemnly.

"So," she said, "I want to thank you for giving him the advice that you did. He and I talked it over, and we decided he's going to take some paid vacation this week." She studied me. "He's still a police officer, on department payroll. He can't talk directly to any suspects. Except his girlfriend, of course, but he can't talk to her about the *case* at all. But he can come here to visit you, as a friend, and if he happens to notice anything interesting, well . . . the two of you can confer, and you can bring it to me. Got it?"

Warmth filled me. "Got it."

She nodded brusquely. "Now that we've got that settled, I guess it's my turn to be grumpy like McNearny and tell you to stay off my turf and out of my cases." But her eyes sparkled, and she gave me a wink. "I think that's what a lead detective is supposed to do."

"Understood, Detective," I replied with a smirk. "Off the record, do you have anything interesting for me? Is there anything tying the two murders together?"

She chuckled. "I'll say. Two stabbings in twenty-four hours in the same hospital is probably enough to tie them together in and of itself—*and* the victims were both stabbed in the carotid artery, which is another big piece of evidence."

"Okay." I scribbled a few notes.

"*Aaaaaand*," she said, drawing out the word, "the killer left a note at the second crime scene."

"Whoa!" I gasped aloud, delighted by this stroke of luck. "Really? What did it say?"

Notes could be gold mines of evidence! Fingerprints, handwriting, turns of phrase, hints about motive and identity.

"*They'll never hurt anyone again,*" Deb replied, rubbing her temples. "That's it. I'm having it checked for prints, ink, that sort of thing. We'll see if we can find out anything else."

"Hmm." I chewed the end of my pen. "That hints at a motive, but doesn't spell it out. But certainly suggests the same person was responsible for both deaths."

"It makes sense with my working theory, which—I'm sorry to say—is that McNearny's girl is the guilty party. Both men hurt her—one jilted her and the other betrayed her."

It made sense as a theory, but McNearny's anguished face flashed through my mind. *I know her. And I know murder cases,* he'd said.

I hesitated, my thoughts circling back to Nurse Bindi.

I'd do anything for my little NICU angels.

"What are you thinking?" asked Deb, slumping back against the wall.

"I do . . . have one other theory," I said slowly. "I hate to say it, though."

"Say it." She scooted back up onto the counter. "We're just tossing around ideas here, not storming out to arrest anyone."

"It's seemed like there's some . . . professional tension around here."

Deb chuckled darkly. "Looks like it."

"Renee hinted to me that it was a possibility some NICU babies had died due to Samuel's negligence. And Dr. Phillips hadn't endeared himself to the other staff. Did I tell you about the fight my NICU nurse had with Dr. Phillips while I was in labor? Before Samuel died?"

She squinted at me. "Yeah, that sounds familiar. Refresh me on what she said, exactly?"

I closed my eyes and summoned the memory. "*Cory, I swear on my great-uncle's grave, you're going to burn in hell for all the wreckage you leave in your wake. You and Samuel both. I'm sick of looking at you!*"

Deb whistled and tossed the flask in the garbage can. "Well, maybe I'm back on the clock, after all. That'd be quite a coincidence for her to say that so soon before both men were murdered. Do you have any idea what kind of wreckage she was talking about?"

I rubbed my eyes, exhausting overtaking me. "What . . . what if something happened to a patient? Either a new mom or a NICU baby, or both. Maybe Bindi got too close to them and blamed Samuel and Dr. Phillips for their death?"

Deb nodded slowly. "All right. If we find out about any suspicious NICU deaths, we should probably look into family members, too."

"But the cameras malfunctioned," I pointed out. "We don't have any footage from the time of the murder."

"Yeah, yeah, yeah." Deb waved a hand. "Which means it was an inside job. Either the killer works here or the killer paid off someone who works here. What's the name of the nurse that seemed to have beef with the doctor?"

"Bindi. I . . . I don't remember a last name."

"First name's fine," Deb grunted. "Her name's Bindi—how many of those can there possibly be in the NICU?"

With a chuckle, I said, "It's not like she's a Jessica or a Lindsay."

Deb rubbed her temples. "All right, I'll look into some background on her tonight or first thing tomorrow, depending on how sober I feel when I get home."

"I'll see if I can get Bindi talking next time I visit the babies." I tapped my pen against the notepad and yawned. "Maybe she'll let her guard down and say something important . . . something that incriminates her or that points to a particular case that she might want revenge for."

CHAPTER FIFTEEN

I slept solidly that night—no doubt thanks to the steady supply of pain medicine. One advantage to a C-section.

When I woke up close to noon, an idea sparked in my mind. If I eased back into my maternity clothes and walked confidently, would the nurses stop me from leaving the maternity ward?

Could I sneak into the NICU to visit Jim and the babies—and maybe even Nurse Bindi?

Worth a try.

It's not like this was the highest-stakes sneaking I'd done while investigating a case. If I could skulk through the French ambassador's house, surely, I could sneak through a hospital.

Carefully, I pulled on a loose-fitting dress and stuffed my feet into my flip-flops.

I peeked out my door, hoping to find the hallway momentarily empty. But instead, Mama Tina was walking past my room, holding a box.

"Oh!" I exclaimed. "Hi, Mama Tina!"

She smiled at me. "Hello, dear. How are you feeling today?"

"Still sore, but doing better every day—and even more importantly, the twins are doing better every day! I'm hoping we'll be discharged tomorrow."

If I were being completely honest, I wouldn't mind *one* extra day in the hospital . . . if it would help me solve the case, plus it was nice to have the extra help taking care of the babies.

But at the same time, I ached to be home with the boys and Laurie.

She shifted the box to her hip. "I'm so glad. It's always a relief to get moms and babies back home to normal life, and"—concern washed over her face—"especially now, with all this bad business going on."

I seized my opening. "Yes," I said, affecting a distant expression. "It's been so tragic and strange. Two doctors murdered!"

She nodded grimly, opened her mouth, and closed it again.

"Are you afraid?" I asked softly. "That the killer's not done?"

She tilted her head, as if surprised by my question. "I don't think I'm afraid, no. At least, not for myself. No one with a grudge against Dr. Hall—I mean, Samuel—or Dr. Phillips would have a grudge against me."

That caught my attention. I leaned back against the wall and studied her. "Does that mean you have an idea of who *might* have had a grudge against them?"

She grimaced, looked up and down the hall, and whispered, "Let's not do this here."

Why does she want to talk to me in secret? As far as she's concerned, I'm just another patient. But I wasn't going to let this opportunity slip away.

I raised my voice a little louder and said, "Would you mind taking me out to the hospital gardens, Mama Tina? I'm going absolutely crazy in here. I think I need some contact with nature and some sunlight."

She beamed at me. "I'd be delighted. Let me go get a wheelchair for you."

A couple minutes later, she returned with a wheelchair instead of the box she'd been carrying. She wheeled me past the receptionist's desk and out the automatic doors to a lush garden.

I lifted my face to welcome the warm beams of sunlight and let out a happy sigh.

We reached a fountain with a statue of a horse in the middle, and she parked my wheelchair and sat down heavily on the lip of the fountain. The fragrant smell of flowers blew past us on a sudden breeze.

"The running water should cover our conversation," she said softly, her voice husky. "I . . . I'm sorry, this is intrusive, but when I was passing by your room, right before I took you to the NICU that time, I overheard you talking. You're a private investigator."

My heart pounded a little faster. So *that* was why she'd wanted to talk.

"Yes," I replied softly. "Well, not officially—I'm still in training, getting my required hours, but I've solved a few cases."

"I . . . looked you up online last night—I'm sorry, I know I shouldn't have. But it sounds like you're one of the best in the city."

I bit my lip, trying to decide how much to tell her. "I've learned to trust my instincts at this point."

No point downplaying my record, since she'd looked it up.

She let out a sigh and wiped a hand over her face. "Everyone's afraid, Miss Kate. Everyone's jumpy. I'm worried that patients are getting substandard care because the doctors and nurses are afraid the killer is lurking around every corner."

I pursed my lips. "We'll solve the murders as quickly as we can. Was there . . . something you wanted to tell me? About someone here at the hospital who might have held a grudge against the victims?"

She hesitated and scrunched up her face. "This feels so wrong . . . like I'm ratting out my coworkers."

I leaned forward, wincing a little at a twinge of pain in my surgery site. "Mama Tina, we'll investigate any leads you give us, but just because we get a name doesn't mean they're guilty. We look at a *lot* of people as a case unfolds. Besides, the killer has struck twice already. What if they strike again? You might be *protecting* your coworkers by telling me about your suspicions."

She let out a long sigh. "Well, if you'd told me a week ago that two men would be murdered in the hospital, I wouldn't have been surprised to find out it was those two. They were friends, although I think it was more about the fact that they liked chasing skirts together than that they really felt deep friendship for each other. You know what I mean?"

I tilted my head, frowning, thinking back to my C-section, when we'd found out about the first murder. Docta C *had* seemed to go a shade pale, but he hadn't dropped his brusque professionalism except to express concern for Nurse Renee.

That made sense if Samuel was a distant friend or a friendly acquaintance but not someone the doctor really felt close to.

Mama Tina continued, "Now, they weren't the best-liked doctors here, not by a long shot. And there's more than one way they might have angered someone. I imagine you've already found out about the whole situation with Miss Renee, your nurse."

"That she used to date them?" I asked.

With a nod, Mama Tina said, "And they were terrible ladies' men. The worst of anyone here. So, I'm sure you're following those leads . . ."

"Do you know why Samuel's medical license was suspended?" I blurted.

"DUI," she said, her lips pursed in disapproval. "On his way home from a double shift at the hospital. But"—her voice dropped to a conspiratorial whisper—"everyone's assuming he was drunk at work, and that's never made any sense to me. He admitted the DUI to people and let them assume it was alcohol, but why would he have been drinking on a double shift?"

"What do you mean?"

"It seems like it had to be drugs," she said, folding her hands together. "Wouldn't you think? Like . . . amphetamines or something. An upper, not a downer. There was a long period of time—six months or so—where we were short-staffed in the NICU. He picked up a lot of extra shifts . . ."

She glanced side to side and whispered, "To be honest, I think more than was safe for patients. Sometimes it seemed like he was here as much as the baby doctors were—I don't mean pediatrics; I mean the residents just out of med school."

"I see." I tilted my head, thinking. "Residents work a lot of hours, don't they?"

"They used to work twenty-four hour shifts sometimes," said Mama Tina, shaking her head. "That's not allowed anymore—and it's been a few years since it was—but they still work them too many hours, and it's bad for patients. Sixteen-hour shifts are pretty common."

I whistled. "I don't think I'd want a doctor who'd been on the clock for fifteen hours."

"*I* certainly wouldn't," said Mama Tina. "Anyway, a while back—a few months before the DUI, maybe? I don't remember exactly—a baby died in the NICU that probably shouldn't have died."

My heart flew to my throat, and I wanted to puke. The sudden panic squeezing my heart wanted reassurance that my babies would come home safe and sound with me.

She continued, "The parents settled with the hospital. I don't know all the details, but I'm under the impression that the hospital's insurance paid out some money without admitting to any particular negligence, because of how short-staffed we'd been. They didn't want it to go to court."

"Okay," I said slowly.

"There was a NICU nurse who'd just loved that baby. She wasn't at work when he died, and I think she blamed herself for not being here. But she also blamed Samuel."

My ears perked up. This fit perfectly with my theory! "What nurse?"

Mama Tina bit her lip, and she said, "Bindi Love. Now, I like Bindi. I don't really think she's a killer. But . . . the whole thing troubles me, and that was one idea I had."

Nurse Bindi! Who is taking care of my babies right now!

Despite the suspicions I'd been harboring, my voice came out strangled. "Did Bindi Love hold a grudge against Dr. Phillips, too?"

Mama Tina chuckled darkly. "Like I said, Dr. Phillips didn't endear himself to most anyone here. I know Bindi thought he tried to keep recovering moms of the NICU babies in the maternity ward too much, especially after C-sections. Didn't allow them enough time with their newborns."

"Wow." I let out a long breath that sounded like a hiss. "Is there anything else you think I should know?"

She looked down at the concrete walkway. "This isn't the best work environment—but don't let the hospital know I said that, or they might fire me—and everyone's competitive with each other. Sometimes it feels like I'm on the set of *Grey's Anatomy* rather than in a real healthcare setting with professionals who are bound to take the best care of their patients. There's another doctor . . . Dr. Hobbs."

"An OBGYN?"

Mama Tina studied me grimly. "That's right. I think he's a good doctor, for the most part. But he had differences of opinion with Dr. Phillips, and he almost got into a physical fight with Dr. Hall—Samuel—once. I don't know what that whole situation was about, but it might be worth looking into."

Leaning back in my chair, I said, "All right. Thinking of all the angles here—of every reason you can think of that someone might have targeted both of these men—is there anyone else who you think might be a target?"

She seemed to consider this, then shrugged. "Not that I can think of. Maybe one of the bureaucrats—hospital administrators, you know. Especially if it was about that NICU baby. But I don't know of any other doctors, at least in maternity and the NICU, who are such notorious womanizers or who have so much tension with the other staff. I think—I hope—that the killer's done."

I fervently hoped she was right. The note had said, *They'll never hurt anyone again.* Maybe that meant the killer had finished what he or she had set out to do.

But I still had to catch them. Samuel and Docta C may have been odious men and bad doctors, but that didn't justify murder.

"Thank you for telling me all this," I said. "This is really helpful and confirms some theories I'm working on. Is there anything else you think I should know?"

She shook her head slowly. "I think that's it. Should I . . . should I tell the police? I thought about calling them, but I don't actually know anything . . . I just have suspicions. I don't want to file a report that turns out to be false."

"In a murder investigation, you can always tell the police your suspicions," I assured her. "You don't have to wait until you have something concrete. Detective Deb Fisher is the lead on this case, and I know she'd love to hear what you have to say."

"Okay." Mama Tina nodded, looking thoughtful. "I'll call her on my break."

"And I'll start looking into the leads you've given me." A wild idea bloomed in my mind. "Hey! Do you have access to the staff rooms?"

She held up her badge. "Of course. Why?"

“I have an idea.”

CHAPTER SIXTEEN

Mama Tina swiped her badge and grumbled under her breath.

Beep, beep! The sensor light shone green, and the automatic unlocking mechanism buzzed.

I nervously swept my hands over the XL scrubs Mama Tina had found for me, then grabbed hold of the door handle and pulled.

My gaze swept over the room, and I found myself surprised.

I'm not sure what I'd expected—maybe a windowless locker room with a couple of small tables. But this was a large, spacious lounge, with multiple rooms, comfortable chairs, and pleasant natural light. It smelled of antiseptic, like the rest of the hospital, but otherwise could have been a trendy study zone on a college campus.

Several pairs of nurses sat chatting at the tables, and a young woman in a doctor's coat snored, slumped in a cushy chair.

"Act natural," murmured Mama Tina. "As long as no one recognizes you, they won't ask questions if you're dressed in scrubs and act like you belong here."

"Where are the cubbies?" I whispered.

"Turn right," she replied quietly.

Together, we walked right—well, she walked, I still toddled, my stride now encumbered from the sutures. We ducked behind a long wall. Once we were out of sight of the other staff, I relaxed a little. We reached the wall of cubbies, and I scanned them. About half of the cubbies were filled with personal possessions—purses and coats, sometimes an outfit.

Three cubbies, in particular, caught my attention—the bags inside had a masculine look, the sort of thing that I could imagine Samuel or Docta C carrying. I reached out and grabbed one bag, opening it up and rummaging through its contents.

A wallet! I flipped it open and looked at the driver's license.

Johnson, Jameson Drew.

I tossed the wallet back in the bag and shoved the bag into the cubby.

"Could you grab that one?" I asked, pointing to a bag just above my head.

It wasn't too high—I could have grabbed it myself if it weren't for my C-section stitches.

Mama Tina pulled down the satchel and handed it to me. I dug through it, looking for a wallet. *No luck.*

But then my fingers closed around a phone. I pulled it out, clicking it on.

The screensaver showed a picture of Docta C in a nightclub setting, a beautiful young woman on each arm.

"Gotcha," I murmured. "Goodness, what a jerk."

The phone was down to four percent battery, and it required a four-digit pin to access.

I frowned at the screen, then asked Mama Tina. "You wouldn't happen to have a flashlight on you, would you?"

"No, sorry."

I snapped my fingers. "Oh! I have an idea. I brought my phone with me!"

I pulled out my phone, turned on the flashlight feature, and handed it to Mama Tina.

"Shine it on his screen," I whispered.

She shone the light steadily, and I held his phone horizontal, right at eye level. "There we are," I whispered as the flashlight revealed a set of smudged fingerprints. "I think the numbers in the pin are 1280."

"So, that's the pin?" Mama Tina asked, her jaw dropping.

"Well, not necessarily in that order," I replied, "but some combination of those numbers. Probably."

The battery dropped to three percent. "And we have to plug this in," I added.

I glanced at the charging port on Docta C's phone, satisfied that my phone charger would work. Then I tucked his phone in my pocket, took mine back from Mama Tina, and fired off two identical texts, one to Deb and one to Galigani: *What was Cory Phillips's birthday?*

We slipped out of the staff lounge and headed back up the hallway to my room. By the time we reached it, Deb had replied, *August 12, 1986. Why?*

"Bingo!" I whispered. August 12—08/12.

"What?" asked Mama Tina, closing the door behind her.

"Figured out the passcode."

I grabbed Docta C's phone and tapped *0812*. The screen unlocked.

What should I check first? His text messages, I decided. Those would likely tell me how many women he'd been stringing along recently.

I opened his texts and scanned the messages. A woman's name caught my attention: *Sarah*. I glanced through that conversation but realized after about ten seconds that she must be his sister.

Who else?

There was a pair of appointment reminders, a group chat called Bar Hoppers, and . . .

Samuel Hall.

Docta C had texted Samuel shortly before Samuel's murder! I opened the thread, my heart pounding, and started reading the messages in reverse order.

Cory Phillips: *Yeah, found an excuse, lol. Usually can with twins.*

Samuel Hall: *Gonna get that extra $$$?*

Cory Phillips: *Greene had the right idea. I need a trip to Europe. At least a twin birth just walked in.*

Cory Phillips: *Yeah, got a job offer, but I turned it down. $ is worse, and hours are just as bad.*

Samuel Hall: *Did you hear back from the hospital in LA?*

Cory Phillips: *I swear, these hours are going to be the death of me. I'm exhausted.*

I stared at the screen and read the messages through again, this time in their proper order, once, twice, then three times. I thought I was going to be dizzy.

Twin birth? He had to be talking about *me*!

What does "gonna get that extra $$$?" mean? A horrifying suspicion took hold of me.

Surely not . . .

"Are you all right, dear?" asked Mama Tina. "You look pale. Do you need me to get a doctor?"

"No." I took a shaky step toward the bed and sank down to sit on it. Then I looked up at Mama Tina. "Do . . . do doctors make more money on C-sections than they do on . . ."

She gasped aloud, grabbed the phone from me, and read through the messages. "He didn't! Why, that good-for-nothing, low-life . . . I should have killed him myself!" She looked from the screen to me and back at the screen. "Yes . . . they . . . they do get paid more for C-sections."

I felt sick to my stomach. *What a violation.*

Mama Tina rested a gentle hand on my shoulder. "There, there. Just breathe, my dear. Just breathe."

For a heady moment, I wanted to drop the case—to walk away and let the murderer get away with it.

What terrible, terrible men.

I bit down on my tongue until I tasted blood, inhaling and exhaling great gasps of air and slowly gathering myself. When the dizziness finally subsided, I glanced up at Mama Tina and whispered, "Well, that was quite a discovery."

My C-section stitches ached more acutely now that I knew the surgery had been unnecessary. Had he lied about the baby being breech?

I closed my eyes and pictured the moment. Docta C had been the only person with a good view of the ultrasound screen.

Mama Tina's mouth was set in a grim line. "I'm so sorry that he did that."

What if he put my babies at risk?

"I . . . I have to go to NICU," I said finally. "I have to see my husband. I—"

My voice cracked, and Mama Tina enfolded me in a soft hug. "I'll take you there right away."

She helped me sit in the wheelchair and wheeled me out of the maternity wing with the casual confidence of a territorial cat.

When we reached the babies' room, I found Jim and my mom there, each of them holding one of the boys.

Jim's face lit up when he saw me, but a moment later his expression faded to concern. "What's wrong, Kate?"

Mama Tina parked my wheelchair. "She's had a shock," she said. "But she'll be all right. Everyone will be all right."

Then, in a low grumble, she added, "At least every decent soul in this hospital."

"Darling?" Mom asked, alarmed. "What happened? You can tell us."

I made eye contact with Mom, then Jim, tears brimming in my eyes. "I . . . was snooping around on the case. Mama Tina was helping me. She knows I'm a PI."

Jim nodded, his face a picture of concern.

The baby in Mom's arms started fussing, and she bounced him up and down to soothe him.

I opened my mouth again, trying to find the words. "We found Dr. Phillips's phone." I glanced at Mom. "He was the one who performed the C-section on me." Then, the words came all at once. "I read a text message thread he had with Samuel, the other victim. They were such . . . such terrible people, and it turns out that I didn't need a C-section! Dr. Phillips made up an excuse to give me one because it made him more money!"

"He did what!" Mom screeched.

Jim looked like he was about to hit the ceiling. His face reddened, and he abruptly handed the baby to Mama Tina. Unfettered rage gleamed in his eyes. I didn't think I'd ever seen him this angry.

But when he spoke, each word was tightly controlled, "He gave you unnecessary surgery, against your wishes, to make more money. And he bragged about it to a friend, breaking patient confidentiality?"

My jaw dropped. I hadn't considered that angle. "Well . . . yeah, I guess. I don't know if that part's strictly illegal—Samuel worked here and no doubt would see medical records, but . . ."

"But that still doesn't give him any right to send a friend text messages about it," he hissed. "Do you still have that phone?"

I showed him the text message thread, and a vein pulsed in his forehead. He clenched his hands into fists.

"We're going to sue," he said, enunciating each word. "We're going to sue the hospital, the doctor's estate, and every person here who knew what he was up to."

The screen went black, and I realized dully that I'd forgotten to charge it.

Mom bounced the baby more furiously—for once in her life, she'd been rendered speechless.

"I'm calling the police," Jim mumbled, whipping out his phone.

He started dialing 911, and I grabbed his arm. "Wait," I whispered. "Don't call 911. That . . . that becomes public record. Call Deb."

After a brief hesitation, he nodded and made the call. Deb picked up after two rings—I could just barely make her voice out through the line.

"Jim? What's up?"

"Deb." His voice was still clipped, like he was barely containing his rage. "We have a situation."

"Is Kate all right?" Deb demanded.

"Yeah. Sorry. I mean, she's not hurt. Well . . . I mean, she is, but not like—"

"You're scaring me."

Jim's gaze landed on me, fierce and protective. "She found out that the doctor pretended she needed a C-section so he could bill the insurance at a higher rate."

There was a long silence, and then Deb let loose a string of profanities so colorful my mom covered the baby's ears.

"Yeah," said Jim. "My thoughts exactly."

I reached for the baby in Mama Tina's arms, nestled him in my lap, and checked his tiny arm bracelet. "Hello, Primus," I whispered, memorizing his handsome little face. Warmth filled my heart and I noted that Primus' eyes were just a shade darker than his brother's.

"Put me on speakerphone," Deb said.

Jim clicked a button and said, “You’re on speaker.”

“Kate?” Deb said, much louder.

“Yeah?” I replied weakly.

“How’d you find out?”

“Well . . . I snooped through Dr. Phillips’s phone.” I didn’t look up. I just studied my baby’s face.

She let out a heavy sigh. “Okay, well I can’t send a beat cop out to take your statement, then, for obvious reasons, but I am going to need to take that phone into evidence. Where’d you find it?”

“Cubbies in the staff lounge,” I said tightly.

“Okay, we’ll take it into evidence, along with anything else in that cubby, and once we’ve catalogued it, I’ll send the case over to our fraud department. If the doctor were still alive, I’d charge him with assault.” She sighed loudly. “Anyone else know about this?”

“The orderly who helped me snoop.” I offered Mama Tina a soft smile. “She’s still here.”

“Can she hear me? What’s her name?”

“I’m Tina Henderson, ma’am,” Mama Tina replied.

“All right, Tina Henderson,” she said. “Thanks for your help, and don’t tell a soul about any of this, okay?”

“I won’t,” promised Mama Tina. “My lips are sealed.”

“I’m serious,” Deb insisted. “Especially no one at the hospital—because that would constitute interfering with an investigation, got it?”

“Got it,” Mama Tina replied.

“All right. Anything else?” asked Deb.

“When can I sue the hospital for everything they own?” grumbled Jim.

“Not until after we catalogue the evidence in the phone. Keep all this to yourselves, and I’ll talk to you later.”

CHAPTER SEVENTEEN

Mama Tina left me with Mom and Jim, and I tried my best to put the whole terrible C-section business out of my head. I didn't want the twins to sense my turmoil.

"When will Nurse Bindi be here?" I asked.

Jim yawned. "I think her shift starts at like four, maybe? I don't remember. But it shouldn't be too long."

I glanced at the clock: it was just past two.

"Should we think more about names?" I asked, running my fingertip along Primus's tiny toes.

Mom found her voice again, though her tone lacked its usual jubilation. "I like the Roman theme you have going with their nicknames," she said.

Jim and I exchanged looks, and I rolled my eyes. I'd hoped Mom wouldn't find out about the nicknames. Was she about to suggest we keep *Primus* and *Secundus*?

"But they're not your first and second children," she said, "they're your first and second *boys*."

"Okay," I said slowly. *Where is she going with this?*

"What about Secundus and Tertius?" she asked. "That means *second* and *third*."

Jim chuckled, seeming to relax a little, like he, too, was letting go of the C-section thing—for now. "I think that would only work if Laurie's name was *Prima*—that's the feminine version of Primus."

Mom nodded solemnly. "I thought of that, too. It's a fair criticism."

I pressed my lips together to suppress a smirk.

"What about Romulus and Remus?" Mom asked, her face devoid of even a trace of irony. "The founders of Rome!"

"Hmm." Jim tilted his head. "That's an idea. What do you think, Kate?"

I stared at him, trying to figure out if he was being serious. The gleam in his eyes told me he thought the idea as preposterous as I did.

"Such regal names for such tiny babies," I said as a peace offering, so Mom wouldn't think I was rejecting her suggestions out of hand. "But I want the names to pair well with *Laurie*, you know? It sounds like a mismatch to say, 'These are my children: Laurie, Romulus, and Remus.'"

"Hmm." Mom tilted her head, as if thinking. "True."

"Jim and I did both like *Lucas*, though. That sounds kind of Roman, and I think it pairs well with Laurie."

Mom nodded and snapped her fingers. "If you have a Laurie and a Lucas, you'll need another *L* name. What about . . . Lucius?"

I looked down at the baby in my arms. "Lucas and Lucius?"

"Oh, you're right," Mom said, "those names are similar. What about Linus?"

"Like the *Peanuts* character?" Jim pulled up a chair next to me, took Secundus from Mom, and sat down with him.

As I looked into the eyes of both of my babies, my heart melted all over again. "We'll be home soon," I whispered. "Whatever names you end up with. We'll be home safe and sound, all five of us together as a family."

"Will you be discharged tomorrow?" Mom asked. "That sweet nurse said the babies are almost ready to go home."

I glanced up at her. "It's possible, but might be one more day. I . . . I might try to stay one more day to solve the case."

Mom hesitated for a long moment, her gaze conflicted. Then she said softly, "Are you sure that's what you want, dear? No one would blame you for walking away from the case now, after finding out what sort of person your doctor was."

"I agree." Jim rested a hand on my knee. "I want you out of this place as soon as possible."

Part of me agreed, too.

A dark wounded part of my heart thought Docta C and Samuel had gotten what was coming to them, that maybe I didn't want to bring the killer to justice.

But McNearny's anguished face flashed in my mind.

"McNearny came to see me today," I replied. "It turns out he's dating my nurse, and she's Deb's chief suspect."

Mom breathed in sharply. "Oh."

I kissed Primus on the forehead and said, "After everything McNearny and I have gone through together on cases . . . it feels like I owe it to him to see this through, if I can."

Jim studied me, then nodded. "I understand. We'll make it work. Just . . . promise me you'll be careful."

I leaned forward and kissed him. "I always am."

AT TWO THIRTY, I went back to my room to take another nap. Not long after, a new doctor came to check on me. "How are you feeling?" he asked.

He seemed about fifty, and his bedside manner was warm and humble—a huge contrast to Docta C.

Just in case this new doctor was thinking of discharging me, I put a hand to my forehead and let out a sigh. "Not as well as yesterday, I'm afraid."

He nodded seriously. "Progress isn't always a straight line, but let me take a look at your chart, just to make sure I'm not missing anything. What are your symptoms today? I'm Dr. Hobbs, by the way."

Dr. Hobbs! Mama Tina had said Dr. Hobbs had differences of opinion with Docta C—and he'd almost gotten into a fistfight with Samuel!

He logged into the computer and pulled up my records.

I told him about pain in my surgical site, fatigue, nausea—anything I could think of to make sure I wasn't discharged early.

At the end of my monologue, he frowned. "Hmm. Well . . . I have to admit, I was hoping to discharge you tomorrow—patients rest more comfortably at home—but you might be here a couple days. We can play that by ear. We certainly have the space."

I squinted at him, surprised at that last statement. "Oh, you do? I heard some nurses complaining about being overworked."

"That was before someone killed two people in the maternity ward." He shook his head sadly. "A number of patients abruptly switched—went to different hospitals for their deliveries yesterday and this morning. That's not ideal—continuity of care from pregnancy to postpartum is best—but I can't say I don't understand it."

"If you think I need to stay, that's fine." I folded my hands in my lap and tried to look prim and proper so he wouldn't sense me scheming. "But . . . do you think I could be given a little more freedom? I'd like to be able to go see my babies in the NICU whenever I want, and maybe walk the hospital grounds when I feel up to it." I grinned widely, willing him to agree.

"Those babies need their mother," he replied with a satisfied nod. "You're welcome to go over there as often as you want. As far as the hospital grounds . . ." He tilted his head, then shrugged. "I suppose that's all right, but take someone with you if you go outside—your husband or your mom or someone. Does that work for you?"

"It does," I said, a demure smile on my face.

He left, closing the door behind him. A split second later, I realized he'd left his computer logged in.

My breath caught in my throat. *This is my chance to snoop!*

I climbed out of bed, glanced nervously at the door, then marched to the computer. First, I tried to see if I could access any of the hospital's HR files. Had anyone lodged complaints about Docta C . . . especially anything to do with unnecessary C-sections?

Docta C? More like Docta C-section.

But after a few clicks through the computer's menus, I realized I was out of luck. Evidently the doctors didn't have access to personnel files—which, I acknowledged begrudgingly, made sense.

Still, maybe I could find a clue in the medical records of Dr. Phillips's patients. I pulled up a list of his recent patients and noted the percentage of C-sections.

"Forty-five percent?" I whispered, raising an eyebrow. That seemed *way* too high.

I did the same thing for Dr. Greene, my normal OBGYN, and Dr. Hobbs, the new replacement. They were at twenty-two percent and twenty-six percent, respectively.

If I hadn't read the text messages, I might have imagined an innocent explanation—maybe that Dr. Phillips accepted a higher percentage of complex cases that were more likely to progress to C-sections.

But with those terrible messages buzzing in the back of my mind, I snapped photos of the evidence on my cell phone.

"What else?" I whispered.

I pulled up the NICU doctors and looked at the list of Samuel's former patients. I sorted the list by the grimmest of outcomes:

deceased. Quickly, I tabbed through it, looking for any hints that Samuel had been negligent.

There weren't very many deaths—the mortality rate was no higher than among the patients of other doctors, and nothing about the cases seemed suspicious for negligence. All those poor, lost babies had been born very prematurely—the sort of cases that proved a challenge for any doctor.

I rubbed my eyes.

What am I missing? I expanded my search, trying to figure out which baby Mama Tina had been talking about.

Finally, I found a case that struck me as strange—the death of a little girl, Anna Jerome, three months earlier. She'd been born just two weeks early, and her birth weight wasn't especially low. I read through the case notes, tears springing to my eyes.

Anna had been brought to the NICU with head trauma after a nurse fell and dropped her right after delivery. The notes were terse, but it looked like the nurse had collided with another staff member and lost her grip on Anna. But none of the names were relevant to my investigation—Anna had been delivered by Dr. Greene and gone into the NICU *after* Samuel's suspension. The nurse who'd dropped her had resigned shortly afterward.

I let out a long breath, trying to compose myself. On my phone, I searched the internet for Anna's name. There had been a small story about it in the city paper, and it looked like the hospital had rapidly settled with the parents for an undisclosed sum of money.

Could Anna's parents have been out for revenge? But why target Docta C and Samuel?

Still, something about the case tingled at the edge of my senses. My intuition told me that, somehow, it was significant—one piece of this complicated puzzle.

I snooped around a little more, but nothing else felt important. With a sigh, I navigated back to my own chart and put the computer to sleep.

Next stop: the NICU.

I ran a brush through my hair, left my room, and held my breath as I walked past the nurses. *My doctor gave me permission to roam freely,* I wanted to yell every time someone glanced my way.

But no one challenged me as I left the maternity ward.

When I reached the NICU, Jim snoozed in a chair next to the incubators, and Mom was nowhere in sight. Nurse Bindi was bent over Secundus, talking in a high-pitched voice.

My thoughts flitted to Anna's parents, and a sudden swell of emotion overwhelmed me. *What a tragedy.*

"Rise and shine, sweet boy," Nurse Bindi cooed. "Did you have a good sleep? Are you going to get to go home very soon?"

I rapped on the doorframe. "Hey!" I called.

Nurse Bindi turned around and waved at me with an enthusiastic smile. "I thought I might see you here this afternoon!" she chirped. "Especially now that you're in Dr. Hobbs's care."

"What do you mean?"

A new suspicion tingled in the back of my mind. Why *had* Docta C insisted I stay put in the maternity ward?

She pursed her lips. "Well, I won't speak ill of the dead, so let's just say that Dr. Hobbs is more attentive to the needs of babies and new moms. Dr. Phillips had some . . . firm ideas that I can't say I agreed with."

I bit down on my tongue as another swell of anger pulsed through me. *Why was Docta C so controlling? Would I have gotten more time with the babies if Dr. Greene had been here?*

"Come here," called Bindi, "and hold this little one!"

She gently picked up Primus and handed him to me. It felt so *right* holding him in my arms. "What should your name be?" I whispered. "It seems like we should have named you by now!"

Primus appeared to have no opinion on the subject.

I sat down, still clutching him tightly.

Now's my chance to ask Bindi some questions.

"You're so good at this. How long have you worked here?"

Jim snorted and sat up for a brief moment, smiled at me, and nodded off in the chair.

Bindi chuckled at him and then glanced at me. "Almost twenty years!" she declared. "It's my life's work."

"A lot must change over twenty years."

She adjusted one of the tubes in the incubator. "It does. It's been really amazing to watch. We can save so many more of my babies now—babies born earlier and earlier. It does my heart good whenever I watch a hard case—a baby whose survival was touch and go for a long time—go home with her parents."

I paused a moment. "Can I ask you a strange question?"

"I'm sure I've heard it before. No question is strange in the NICU!"

"It's about Dr. Phillips."

At the name *Dr. Phillips*, Jim startled, then opened one eye.

She stiffened a little. "What about him?"

"I feel badly asking this, now that he's dead." I leaned back in the chair, drawing comfort from my baby's presence in my arms. "But . . . it didn't seem like he was your favorite person here."

She whirled around and stared at me. "What about it? What are you suggesting?"

That reaction seemed a little suspicious.

"Nothing!" I exclaimed, eyes wide, trying to defuse her sudden agitation. "It's just . . . I thought I might get honest answers out of you that I haven't been able to get out of the nurses over in maternity. I'm . . . I'm concerned Dr. Phillips might not have given me good medical care."

Her face softened immediately. "I'm so sorry to hear that. Do you mind me asking what happened?"

I blurted, "Do you happen to know if Dr. Phillips did a surprising number of C-sections? More than he should have?"

Her countenance fell. "That's . . . that's not really something I'm supposed to talk about. The liability for the hospital . . ." She looked up, her steady gaze meeting mine, something like defiance shining through. "But I won't deny it."

"I'm sorry the men died," I murmured, "but to hear everyone else around here talk, I get the feeling the hospital might be a much better place with them gone."

"You're not wrong," she said, and I was surprised by the vehemence in her voice. "I'm so sick of people making excuses for him." Her tone turned ironic. "Guess that doesn't matter anymore."

She hesitated, then plunged ahead. "Yes. I thought it was perfectly obvious he did too many C-sections. I reported it, even, but that went nowhere. His C-section rate always seemed a little high to me, but over the last few months, it's absolutely gone off the rails."

She stood up straighter, still defiant.

My phone buzzed with a text message, and I glanced down at the screen, in case it was Deb or Galigani with an update.

But instead, it was from Rachelle—she'd sent a picture of Laurie finger painting, with the message. *Don't worry about a thing! She's having a great time.*

My heart warmed.

I looked back up at Bindi, and her face seemed almost remorseful.

She rubbed her temples. "I really shouldn't have said any of that. I'm just so on edge after everything." She took a deep breath. "Excuse me."

With that, she practically bolted out of the room. Jim and I stared at each other, and he raised a skeptical eyebrow.

"Daaaaarling!" called Mom as she swept through the door. "Sit down! Shouldn't you be resting?"

I shrugged. "The doctor said I should try to walk around some. He even said I could walk outside if I took you or Jim." The hospital air suddenly felt stifling, like the four walls of the room were closing in on me. "Hey, could one of you stay with the babies and one of you take me outside?"

"I'll stay with the babies," Mom said quickly. "They can never have too much grandma time."

Jim stood and stretched. "Yeah," he said, yawning. "Let's go outside, Kate. That will do you some good."

We reached the garden and walked slowly past the fountain. "Do you need to talk through the case?" he asked. "Did Bindi seem . . . off to you back there?"

With a grimace, I replied, "She did seem off. But . . ." I let out a long sigh. "I've been suspicious of her from the beginning, because of that argument I overheard when I was in labor. But my instincts are telling me it wasn't her."

"Because you're more suspicious of Renee?" He bent over and dipped his fingers into the fountain.

I considered the question and watched a lazy cloud float across the sky. "Maybe. But it's not just that. I just don't think it was Bindi, and I can't tell you why, exactly."

"Do you think it was Renee?"

That time, I stopped in my tracks. *Do I think it was Renee?*

"Well," I answered slowly, "I'm not one hundred percent sure. The facts tell us that she's the strongest suspect."

McNearny's words replayed in my mind. *I know her. And I know murder cases. She's a flawed human being, but she's not a killer.*

“I don’t want it to be her,” I finally said, shuffling forward again. “I hope that, at the end of all this, McNearny will be proven right. It’s just—”

Jim ground to a halt and held up a hand, his gaze snapping toward a nearby hedge.

My forehead crinkled, and I mouthed, “What is it?”

He put a finger to his lips and beckoned me forward. I followed him toward the shrubbery and heard a woman’s voice coming from the other side.

“Tris,” the woman pleaded, “I don’t know what to do. I’m panicking!”

It was Renee!

CHAPTER EIGHTEEN

I froze stock-still, listening to Renee's agitated, one-sided conversation. *She must be on the phone.*

"I've been interviewed by the cops like four times!" she exclaimed. "It seems like they're everywhere. And . . . and—" She took a deep breath, like she was trying not to hyperventilate. "Taking time off work will be suspicious, but I can't—I can't keep doing this! It's making me so anxious."

There was a long pause. I whipped out my phone and started recording the conversation.

Renee continued, "But what if they figure out what I did? It wasn't my fault! He . . . he tricked me! He betrayed me! I—"

Another pause.

Finally, Renee said, "Okay, but *I'm* on the record for that. He asked me to talk to the hospital administration for him so he could get away with doing more C-sections! I'm such an idiot. And when I confronted him about it, he threatened me to not tell anyone or I'd be responsible when women died. It's—"

After another long pause, Renee said, "My break's over. I have to go back in. But Tris, I just don't know what to do. We'll . . . we'll talk tonight."

I ended the recording, and Jim and I stared at each other as Renee's footsteps receded.

"Well," he finally said, "I feel bad for McNearny."

"She didn't confess to murder." I sank down to sit on a wooden bench. "But that conversation certainly gives us motive."

Jim sat next to me and rubbed my shoulder. "So, she agreed to somehow help him out with hospital administration, so he could do more C-sections," he said. "Maybe they were getting on his case about the high number of surgeries?"

"That's what it sounded like," I replied. "And then she felt guilty about it? Or got cold feet? And they had a fight and he threatened that she'd be held liable for maternal deaths if she didn't get with the program."

Jim clicked his tongue. "Sure sounds like a motive for murder to me."

I fired off a text to McNearny: *Who is Tris?* I held my breath as I waited for a reply.

It didn't take long. *Um, Renee has a sister named Tris? Is that who you mean?* he texted back.

Yeah, thanks, I replied. I showed Jim the message. "She was talking to her sister."

He wrapped his arm around me, and I slumped against him. Deep sadness welled up inside me.

I'm sorry, McNearny, I thought. *I wish it didn't have to end this way.* But after that conversation, there seemed to be little doubt that the trail would lead us to Renee. We didn't have proof yet, but I couldn't forget what I'd heard.

"But why Samuel?" I murmured. "Why would she have killed Samuel first?"

"To throw us off the trail?" Jim offered. "To disguise her real motive for killing Docta C?"

"That doesn't make any sense." I sat back up, rubbing my burning eyes. "Who kills their ex-fiancé to throw police off their trail? Samuel's death *guaranteed* the police would look more closely at Renee. Her romantic attachment with Docta C was a long time ago and didn't last very long."

"Suppose you're right." Jim cracked his knuckles. "Maybe she . . ."

He trailed off, leaving the sentence unfinished.

I studied him, my face grim. "Even if she's not our murderer, we know that she helped cover up the unnecessary C-sections."

He sighed. "And you'll have to tell McNearny that."

I stared at the ground. "I didn't want to break his heart."

Jim knelt down in front of me and clasped my hands. "You're not breaking his heart, honey. *She's* breaking his heart. You're just being a good friend and a good detective."

A passing breeze ruffled his hair.

I drew his hand to my lips and kissed his fingers. "I suppose the decent thing to do is tell McNearny in person myself, before we take the evidence to Deb. Will . . . will you come with me? You give me strength."

"Honey, I'm at your side whenever you need me, no matter what."

I smiled softly, and he leaned forward and kissed me on the lips, first gently, then fervently.

With a shaky laugh, I pulled back. "Let's go inside." I sent one more text to McNearny: *Come to my hospital room. We need to talk.*

Jim rested his hand on my lower back, and we trudged toward the automatic doors.

My phone pinged with a reply from McNearny: *What's going on, Connolly? You're scaring me a little.*

I bit my lip but didn't reply.

Mama Tina waved at us as she parked a wheelchair in the lobby. "Hello again, Miss Kate!" she called. She left the wheelchair behind and bustled over to us.

"How is everything going?" she whispered. "You know . . . on the case?"

I managed a strained smile. "Do you think you could help me with one more thing?"

She stood up a little straighter. "Of course, Miss Kate. What is it?"

Before I could answer, the automatic doors opened behind us, and a woman breezed in. I glanced backward, and my mouth went dry.

Renee.

But it wasn't Renee. She had darker hair and stood at least two inches taller. But the similarities in their features left me with no doubt: this had to be Renee's sister.

"Hello, Tris!" called Mama Tina pleasantly. "You just missed Renee's break. She's back at work now—just came inside."

Tris shifted her weight from foot to foot. "I need to see her," she said, clipping her words. "It's urgent."

Mama Tina glanced at me, and I grimaced. I took a deep breath and turned toward Tris.

"Can we talk?" I asked.

Confusion flickered across her features. "I'm sorry. Do I know you?"

I took a deep breath, and my C-section site twinged. "I'm a PI looking into the murders of Samuel Hall and Cory Phillips," I said brusquely.

Jim twitched, but I ignored him. This was my chance to question Renee's sister, and I wasn't going to pass that opportunity up, even though I was blowing my cover. Renee would probably be in handcuffs before her shift ended, anyway.

I folded my hands behind my back to hide my hospital bracelet, feeling suddenly grateful that I'd changed into maternity clothes before going to the NICU earlier.

Tris sucked in a sharp breath and closed the distance between us in five rapid strides. "Renee didn't have anything to do with that!" she hissed.

I watched her closely for any telltale signs of lying, but I didn't see any. Which meant Tris was a very good liar.

Or it means . . .

I plunged ahead. "Let's talk out in the garden."

Tris chewed her lip. "I'm worried about Renee. I talked to her a few minutes ago, and she seemed distraught. I live just around the corner, so I came as fast as I could."

"If you think your sister didn't kill anyone," I said evenly. "The best thing you can do is talk to me and help me fill in some missing pieces."

We stared at each other for what felt like an eternity. Tris looked down first. "She *didn't* kill anyone," she insisted. "I'll talk to you. You have to believe me."

I took a step back toward the doors and a wave of dizziness rushed over me. I grabbed at Jim's arm, waiting for it to pass.

Mama Tina jumped to attention. "I'll get you a wheelchair," she said. "Some dizzy spells are to be expected with the pain medicine you're on—and you just had surgery!"

Tris' brows furrowed. "You just had surgery? I thought you were a PI on the case."

I let Mama Tina ease me into the wheelchair. "Both are true," I said, though I fervently wished Mama Tina hadn't said that in front of Tris. "Being in the hospital has left me with lots of time to look into the case."

Mama Tina wheeled me out toward the garden, and Jim and Tris took up the rear.

When we reached the fountain, Mama Tina turned me around and parked the wheelchair.

Tris stopped a few paces away, her arms crossed.

"I'll cut to the chase," I said. "We know that Renee conspired with Dr. Cory Phillips to cover up the fact that he was giving women unnecessary C-sections."

Mama Tina shrieked. "She what?"

Tris' jaw dropped. "No! That's not—"

"And we know that you're aware of it," I added. "There's no point in denying it."

She fell silent, looking from me to Jim to Mama Tina, her face stricken.

Compassion flooded me. I could see how much Tris loved her sister. "There's no saving Renee from the consequences of her actions, but there's a huge difference between medical fraud and murder." I pressed my palms together. "Tris, if your sister is innocent, help us prove it. Tell us what you know so we can piece together the story of what really happened."

She took a step back. "I . . . I don't know what happened! I don't know who killed those doctors. But I know it wasn't Renee." Her blue eyes pleaded with me. "You have to believe me! And she didn't try to defraud anyone, either."

I pulled out my phone and hit *play* on the recording.

Renee's voice came loud and clear through the speaker. "I've been interviewed by the cops like four times! It seems like they're everywhere. And . . . and—"

Tris' nostrils flared. "Where did you get that?" she hissed. "Did you tap her phone?"

Renee's voice continued, "But what if they figure out what I did? It wasn't my fault! He . . . he tricked me! He betrayed me! I—"

"That's not what you think!" cried Tris. "It's not like that!"

"Then what is it like?" I asked.

Her face paled. "A baby died because it got dropped by a nurse."

Anna. I paused the recording.

I'd been right. Anna's death *was* linked to the case.

Tris' hands tightened into fists. "That doctor told her the hospital needed to make some changes. He blamed it—"

Mama Tina took a menacing step forward. "The doctor told her if he didn't do more C-sections, babies would die?" she bellowed, her nostrils flaring.

No wonder Mama Tina was so angry—as a former doula, she was doubtless a big advocate for natural childbirth.

"No!" Tears sprang to Tris' eyes. "But he convinced her that they needed to make changes to keep it from happening again. She . . . she had doubts, but he persuaded her, and she talked to the administrators. Samuel Hall did too. It took weeks and weeks after that for Renee to realize his C-section rate had gone way up."

Her words struck a chord of memory. Earlier that day, Bindi had said that Docta C had started doing *more* C-sections in the last few months.

"She-she got suspicious," Tris stammered. "But she dismissed it at first. Eventually it got so bad that she couldn't deny it anymore, so she confronted him."

"When was that?" I asked.

Mama Tina trembled with barely controlled rage.

Tris closed her eyes. "A week ago."

"And he threatened her?"

Her eyes popped open, and she shook her head. "Not . . . no, not like that. He didn't threaten her—"

I held up the phone to remind her that I still had the recording of the phone call.

She pressed her lips together. "The doctor admitted to it—and laughed at her for caring!"

What? Shock pulsed through me.

Tris continued, "She said she would take it to the hospital administration, and he told her that she'd get fired alongside him, because she'd cooperated earlier. But this was the part that stopped her in her tracks. He said—" Her voice broke, and she burst into sobs.

Jim pulled a package of tissue out of his pocket and offered her one.

She accepted it, crying into the fragile paper.

"Take your time," I said, my tone reassuring. "Deep breaths."

When she recovered herself, she took a deep, shuddering inhale. "He said that he'd done a few extra C-sections, but that if the . . . if the hospital cracked down on C-sections and made doctors afraid to do them, that—that women would die!"

Mama Tina scoffed. "That's absurd. Any good doctor knows when to do a C-section."

"Well, Renee was in turmoil about it," spat Tris. "She didn't want to be responsible for anyone's death. It wracked her with guilt—she felt guilty if she said anything and guilty if she didn't."

Tris took another deep breath and blurted, "That's how I know she didn't kill anyone! No matter what you say! Because she was tormented at the idea of causing someone's death, even by accident. She wouldn't have murdered anyone!"

Mama Tina crossed her arms, apparently unconvinced.

I tried to sort through everything Tris had said. The story perplexed me, because it dovetailed so well with other things I'd come across—the case of little Anna Jerome's death, Bindi's statement about Docta C giving more C-sections recently . . .

But that phone call sounded so bad.

Tris continued, "And yes, Renee knows how much this would make her look like a murderer! And how hard it would be to prove that she didn't conspire with those doctors. Why do you think she's so anxious about the story coming out?"

As a private investigator, I'd interviewed a lot of people. And I'd started to develop an instinct for when someone was telling me the truth—or at least what they believed to be the truth.

And I had the sneaking suspicion that Tris believed she was telling the truth.

I held up my hands. "I hear you. Thank you for shedding that light on the situation. Any shred of information we collect might help us clear your sister."

Hope shone in her eyes. "Wait . . . really? You don't think she's guilty?"

With a soft smile, I said, "I don't know who's guilty, Tris. I'm just interested in finding the truth."

When Tris left, I watched her get into her car, and then I turned to Jim and a still-fuming Mama Tina. "We have to solve this fast," I said. "Will Renee have her phone with her during her shift?"

Mama Tina shook her head. "No, phones aren't allowed when we're with patients, and she already had her break. It'll probably be at least four hours before she checks her phone."

With a nod, I said, "Good. That buys us a little time before Tris tells Renee about our conversation."

"As long as Tris doesn't break into the hospital," muttered Jim.

I glanced toward the parking lot. "Looks like she's leaving for now. In any case, we need to work fast. Tris was compelling—"

Mama Tina grumbled under her breath.

I ignored her and continued, "And I think she *believes* everything she said. But that doesn't clear Renee—not by a long shot. Of course, her sister believes in her."

And, of course, her boyfriend believes in her.

Tina let out a long sigh. "I'm being too hard on Miss Renee. I always have liked her, and I hope she didn't do it. It just made me so angry to learn that she knew what Docta C had been doing and didn't say anything." She hesitated. "I'll do a little snooping and see if I can find anything."

"You don't have to do that," I assured her.

She crossed her arms. “You said yourself that we have to solve this fast. If Renee’s the killer, you might be in danger if she gets off her shift and finds out how much you know.”

Jim put an arm around me protectively. “I’m going to be with her every moment from here on out.”

“Still,” Mama Tina murmured, a distant look in her eyes, “I’ll feel better if we can get this case locked away before anyone else has to get hurt.”

CHAPTER NINETEEN

Mama Tina wheeled me back to the lobby.

"Should I drop you off here or take you back to your room?" she asked.

"I can walk the rest of the way to my room," I said, though a wave of fatigue was washing over me again.

I sat on one of the lobby couches and called Deb.

"Yo, Kate. What ya got for me?" asked Deb. "I hope it's something good, because I'm not making a whole lot of progress on my end."

"I'm not sure if I'm making progress or not," I said. "I may have found something, but there's a possibility it's a dead end."

"I'm curious. Tell me more."

I played with a loose thread on the end of my sleeve. "Could you send me the police report for the death of Anna Jerome? She died in the NICU here a few months ago."

"What?" Deb sounded confused. "There wasn't a murder in the NICU. I'd know about that."

"No, she was a baby. A nurse dropped her during the delivery, and they rushed her to the NICU, but she ended up dying."

"Huh," she said. "Yeah, I'll pull that up and send it to you. What's your theory?"

"I'll tell you if it checks out."

"I thought you weren't going to be a lone cowgirl on this one," she said flatly.

"Just trust me on this. It's a . . . delicate situation."

"If you say so." Her voice had turned skeptical. "I'm going to need an update from you soon, though."

"I hope I'll have something to tell you soon."

We hung up, and I stood, feeling vaguely dizzy.

"You ready to go?" Jim looped his arm through mine.

I squeezed his arm, and we headed down the hall toward my recovery room.

When we reached my door, we found a frantic McNearny pacing inside.

"Connolly!" he barked. "Where have you been? What do we need to talk about?"

I glanced at Jim and nodded to the door, and he closed it behind us.

"Sit down, Patrick," I said gently, gesturing to the chair near the bed.

McNearny sank down onto the chair, and I sat near him.

"You send me this alarming text message," he exclaimed, "and then I get here and you're just gone!"

I folded my hands. "Something relevant to the case came up. I had to follow the lead."

"Fine," he said tersely. "What did you want to tell me?"

I opened my mouth, then closed it. *What do I say?*

This conversation had seemed a lot clearer twenty minutes earlier, before I'd heard Tris' version of the story.

But the bottom line was this: even if Tris was telling the truth, Renee had known that Samuel and Docta C had been conspiring to profit off of unnecessary C-sections. Maybe she'd helped them, maybe she hadn't.

But who else would have a murder motive? Maybe Bindi would—but how would Bindi know that Samuel had been involved?

Finally, I said, "That lead I was following . . . it may have thrown some things into doubt. When I texted you, I'd just received some information that implicated Renee in the case, at least at some level."

His Adam's apple bobbed. "What do you mean?"

I sighed. "I wish I hadn't summoned you here, because I just talked to Tris, and there may be a . . . relatively innocent explanation. At least one where Renee got caught up in a situation that felt out of control."

"Are you saying she murdered them?" he squeaked.

"I don't know yet." I reached out and rested a hand on his arm.

"Patrick?" Renee strode into the room, her lips pursed as she looked from her boyfriend to me and back again. I pulled my arm back.

"Renee!" McNearny exclaimed, standing up and hurrying toward her. He pulled her into a hug. "How are you holding up?"

She took a step back and studied me with a frosty glare. "I didn't know the two of you were acquainted."

"Oh. Yeah," McNearny said, wincing. "Kate is, uh . . . a friend, who . . ."

Renee's eyes widened in sudden realization. "Kate Connolly," she whispered. "She's . . . she's that private eye you're always complaining about!"

Uh-oh.

Jim moved to stand next to me protectively.

So much for keeping it a secret until the end of her shift.

Renee crossed her arms and stared daggers at McNearny. "I can't believe this! I was taking care of your PI pet in the middle of a crime scene where *I'm* a murder suspect, and you didn't even have the decency to tell me?"

McNearny opened his mouth, then closed it, then stammered, "M-my love, I wasn't . . . I was trying to protect you! Kate was looking into the case so we could clear your name!"

She whirled on me with a fierce glare. "You were spying on me?" she screeched. Jim stepped in front of me.

McNearny stepped in front of Renee.

"I wasn't spying!" I threw my hands out. "I was following a number of leads."

She ducked around McNearny. "And have you figured out who killed them yet?" she hissed through her teeth.

I crossed my arms. "I'm working on it. But you're certainly acting suspicious right now."

"Kate!" McNearny exclaimed.

Renee clenched her hands into fists.

Mama Tina ran into the room, waving a sheaf of paper. "Miss Kate! There's something you should see!" She stopped abruptly when she saw Renee. Her eyes widened for a moment, but she recovered herself. "Hello, Renee!" she said cheerily, like nothing at all was wrong.

Renee looked from Mama Tina to me to McNearny and finally, again, back to me. "So, you have my coworkers spying on me too." A sob caught in her throat. She turned and locked eyes with McNearny, and a misty expression came over her face. "I'm sorry, Pat," she whispered. "I can't do this."

With another sob, she fled the room.

McNearny stared at the door for several seconds, then ran after her. "Renee!" he yelled. "Renee!"

I rested a hand on my forehead and slumped back across the bed. "I hate this case," I murmured. "I just want to be home with my babies."

Mama Tina took a tentative step toward me. "I'm so sorry I barged in here like that. I just didn't expect her to be . . . right there."

"You didn't know." I sat back up. "What did you find out?"

She offered me the sheaf of paper. "I went looking in the staff cubbies, like we did before, and I found this."

I accepted it from her and began to read the first page. “What is this?” I asked, confused.

“A note, I guess?” She shrugged. “I found it with Renee’s things.”

It was written in a masculine scrawl—the sort of penmanship that looked like it belonged to a doctor. I squinted, trying to make out the words. *Thanks for all your help, darling. Couldn’t have done it without you. I never should have turned you down. -C*

“C? Like Docta C?” I asked.

Jim read over my shoulder. “What does it say? I can’t read it at all.”

I read it out loud, then flipped to the second sheet of paper. It was a printout of a hospital record for a C-section birth, with Docta C listed as the attending physician. I turned the page again. Another record, another C-section. And again. And again. And again.

I looked at Jim, feeling dizzy again. “Are these all C-sections that Renee helped Docta C with?”

His brows knitted together. “I suppose so. Odd that he’d send her this, though. Don’t you think?”

“Maybe it was part of his threat,” offered Mama Tina. “Maybe he wanted her to remember how deep she was in the conspiracy, and that he could ruin her career if she stepped out of line.”

“Maybe . . .” I studied each page again, but it didn’t make any more sense the second time.

My phone buzzed—Deb had emailed me the police report I’d asked for.

I yawned, unable to suppress my utter exhaustion.

“You need to rest, Kate,” said Jim, easing me back down to lie on the bed.

“I don’t have time to rest,” I murmured.

“Well,” he said firmly, “I’m not going to give you any choice in the matter. I’m going to stay right here with you until you’ve rested at least half an hour, and not a minute less. Besides, a lot of your best breakthroughs come when you're focused on something else."

"Wake me up after thirty minutes?" I pleaded.

He kissed me on the forehead. "I promise."

Mama Tina murmured another apology and left the room.

But I didn't fall asleep. I rested with my eyes closed, but the memory replayed in my mind on a loop: Renee sobbing as she fled the room, McNearny calling her name and running after her.

He's in love with her.

Finally, I opened one eye and asked, "How long has it been?"

"Twenty-seven minutes," said Jim with a tired half-smile from where he sat in the chair at my bedside.

"Is that close enough to thirty minutes?" I pleaded.

He crossed his arms, but amusement lit up his features. "Did you not hear me when I said *not a minute less*?"

"I heard you." I sat up. "I just hoped you'd relented. Jim . . . he's in love with her."

Sadness washed over his face. "I know."

I bit my lip. "What if I'm missing something? What if her sister is right and she didn't do any of it?"

"Honey, isn't that wishful thinking at this point?"

I swung my legs over the edge of the bed. "You thought Bindi was the killer like an hour and a half ago!"

He helped me to my feet. "So? We've gotten more information since then."

"I just . . . something about the sister's story got to me. If there's any possibility that Renee is innocent, I owe it to McNearny to chase down the clues."

"Well . . ." he said slowly.

We stood, facing each other in silence for a long breath.

"If it's not Renee." He rubbed the back of his neck. "Does that mean it has to be Bindi?"

I met his gaze. “Not necessarily, but Bindi’s certainly our most likely suspect besides Renee.”

“Why don’t we go back to the NICU, then?” He looped his arm through mine. “If the killer is Renee, you’re probably safer in the NICU than you are in your room—and if the killer is Bindi, you might catch her in a lie.”

“Good point.” We left my room and headed down the hall toward the NICU. Halfway down the hall, I looked down at my feet and muttered, “I’m still waddling. Shouldn’t I be done waddling? I’ve had the babies!”

Jim squeezed my arm. “You’ll be back to normal soon, honey. Just a little more patience.”

“I’m bad at patience,” I said with a sigh.

He laughed aloud. “I’m well aware of that.”

When we reached the NICU, Nurse Bindi was storming out of the room across the hall from the twins’ room. She pulled to a halt when she saw us.

“Kate and Jim!” she exclaimed. “Have they arrested her yet?”

“Arrested who?” I asked, my brow creasing in confusion.

“Renee, of course!” She stamped her foot. “I can’t believe what she did!”

“Do you think Renee killed Samuel and Dr. Phillips?” I asked. Jim and I stopped a few paces from Bindi.

She shrugged, a ferocious expression on her face. “I don’t know who killed those sons of—” She cut herself off abruptly, then continued, “I don’t know who killed them, and I don’t care. But I heard about how Renee helped cover up all those unnecessary surgeries, and I think she should go to jail for it!”

I nodded toward the boys’ room. “Could we talk in there?” I asked softly.

She followed us inside.

Mom was holding one twin and sitting next to an incubator, making faces at the other baby. She shot us a questioning glance, and I gave her a small wave.

Bindi and I sat across from each other on a pair of comfy chairs. Jim stood at my side, a hand resting on my shoulder.

Bindi folded her hands on her lap, but they trembled with uncontrolled rage. She swiped at her eyes, brushing away angry tears that brimmed on her lashes. "I'm sorry," she said, her voice tight. "I shouldn't be losing my temper like this. I'm just so angry. C-sections . . . carry risks. Sometimes they're medically necessary, but most of the time they're not. And he had no right to force that risk on so many of *my babies*. And she had no right to help him with it!"

I inhaled shakily and met her gaze. "You're not wrong. I know that better than anyone."

Gently, she whispered, "I know you do."

After a brief hesitation, I asked, "Who told you about Renee?"

A tear trailed down her cheek. "Mama Tina. She was in agony about it—angry at Renee, of course, but hesitant to *rat her out*, as she phrased it."

I nodded. Mama Tina had expressed that same hesitation when she and I had talked alone in the hospital gardens. She'd even used the phrase *ratting out*—which meant I was pretty sure Bindi was telling the truth.

Something bothered me, tingling on the edge of my mind. I wished Tina hadn't asked Bindi, of all people, for advice. She must not have known Bindi was one of our suspects.

Surely I told her? But I couldn't remember—too much brain fog. *Serves me right for solving a case from the hospital.*

"Go on," I said.

Bindi wiped the tear off her cheek and leaned forward, fists clenched. "Anyway, when she explained that you were a PI working with the police—"

I grimaced.

"—I told her that she needed to tell you everything. Renee needs to go to jail for what she did." Then she scoffed. "Or maybe whoever took out Samuel and Dr. Phillips will take her out, too, before police arrest her."

CHAPTER TWENTY

Did I hear her correctly? Did she just hope—out loud, no less—that Renee would be murdered?

I raised an eyebrow but quickly schooled my features into neutrality.

Bindi looked up and said, "And you know what else? I'm convinced that Docta C didn't want you—and other new moms—to come freely to the NICU after C-sections *because* he was doing so many. He wanted to keep an extra close watch on all of you, because if you developed complications, it would draw attention to his C-section practices." Her voice cracked. "So many babies haven't had their moms with them during really crucial periods in the NICU."

I inhaled sharply at the thought.

"And that's why you need to make sure Renee is arrested," Bindi implored. "This can't ever happen again. I know Docta C's dead, but we need to send a clear message that you won't get away with it if you cooperate in such a scheme. You won't!" She smacked her own leg.

Then she stood. "I'm sorry. I'm losing it. I'll be back later."

With that, she rushed out of the room.

Mom whistled. "Darling, I don't like this," she said slowly. "Word is getting around that you're a private investigator. But you're still recovering! It's one thing for you to get into dangerous scrapes when you can run away on your own two feet. It's another thing when you're barely out of surgery!"

"There was a lot about that conversation I didn't like," I muttered.

Jim took the seat Bindi had fled from, then reached out and grabbed my hands. "Honey, I think we need to get you and the boys out of here. Everything about your interactions with *both* Renee and Bindi were suspicious. I don't know who the killer is, but I'm not comfortable with this hospital."

I locked eyes with Jim first, then Mom. Finally, I said, "Mom, can you have Galigani come and sit with you? We can't leave the babies alone with Bindi, but I don't like the idea of you being here alone with her, either." I squeezed Jim's hand. "Jim will stay with me."

Mom immediately dialed Galigani.

Jim gripped my hand and whispered, "Together."

"Always," I replied with a wan smile.

There was a knock on the doorframe, and a petite nurse poked her head in. "Mrs. Connolly?" she asked.

"That's right." I tilted my head in silent question.

With a grin, she exclaimed, "I'm so glad I found you! It's time for your next dose of pain medicine. Would you mind coming back to maternity with me?"

"Sure," I said, realizing that I was indeed starting to feel pain in my surgery site. The case had distracted me from it, but it was definitely time for my next dose.

I stood on shaky legs, and she said, "Would you like a wheelchair?"

I hesitated.

"That'd be great, thanks," Jim said.

The nurse wheeled me toward the maternity ward, Jim following closely behind. As soon as we left the NICU, the nurse leaned toward me and whispered, "Are you really a private investigator?"

“Word travels fast,” I replied wryly. *Nothing to lose, I suppose.* “Do you have any suspicions about who might have killed Samuel and Dr. Phillips?”

“Oh!” she exclaimed. “Wasn’t it Renee? I thought someone said . . .”

“We’re looking at multiple possibilities.” I set my hands on the armrests. “I just asked Bindi Love, in the NICU, about her thoughts on Renee. She seemed quite . . . vehement.”

“Oh, that doesn’t surprise me,” answered the nurse. “Bindi loves her babies. She’s always like that. Sweet as anything when there’s a baby to cuddle, in a rage when she loses one or when she feels like something’s keeping her from giving them the best of care. She wouldn’t hurt a fly, though.”

“What about Renee?” I asked. “Do you think *she’d* hurt a fly?”

The nurse whistled. “I mean, I wouldn’t have thought so, but if the police think she did it . . . I don’t know what to think, I guess. I don’t know—I watch a lot of true-crime documentaries.”

I covered my mouth to suppress a snort.

“Sometimes it’s the person you’d least suspect, right? So, I guess *maybe* that means it could be Bindi. I just have a hard time imagining it.”

We arrived at my room, and she gave me my pain pill. I studied it, making sure it looked exactly like the other ones I’d taken before I swallowed it.

I’d been poisoned too many times while working cases.

She adjusted the thin blanket over me. “All right, you might be tired for a little while, but hit the call button if you need anything.”

When she left the room, I pulled out my phone and opened up the file Deb had sent me—the police report for the death of Anna Jerome.

This report had more detail than the record I'd found on the hospital computer system, and I read it with equal parts interest and heartbreak.

Anna had been delivered perfectly healthy by my usual OBGYN, Dr. Greene. After Dr. Greene had handed her off to a nurse to get cleaned up and weighed, the nurse had tripped over the . . .

My eyes widened, a new suspicion jolting through me. I kept reading. Finally, when I got to the bottom of the eighth page, I sat up with an audible gasp.

"What is it, honey?" Jim leaned toward me. "Are you okay? Are you hurting?"

I felt no pain. Shock flooded me, then relief.

I reached out and gripped his hand. "I know who killed Samuel Hall and Cory Phillips!"

CHAPTER TWENTY~ONE

I texted Deb and McNearny, asking them to meet me as quickly as possible. Not two seconds later, my phone buzzed. *That was fast.*

I looked at the screen, and my heart leaped into my throat.

It was from Mom: *Come now!*

I showed it to Jim, and he leaped to his feet. "Nurse!" he yelled, running to the doorway. "We need a wheelchair now!"

After the longest ten seconds of my life, he raced back in, pushing a wheelchair. "Stole it from a passing orderly," he gasped out. "Let's go!"

We raced to the NICU as fast as Jim could push me. When we reached the babies' hallway, an enraged scream pierced the ward.

"That's coming from the babies' room!" I yelled, pointing.

Jim doubled his speed, and we careened into the boys' room, the wheelchair almost tipping over.

I gasped aloud.

Mom and Bindi were standing, arms extended wide, in front of the incubators, as if protecting the babies.

And Renee was crawling across the floor, toward the doorway. She looked up at me and rubbed her temple. "You have to help me! She's crazy!"

"Stay away from my NICU babies!" Bindi screamed.

Then Mama Tina stalked out from the corner of the room, brandishing a mop handle at Renee.

"Mama Tina!" I yelled. "What are you doing?"

Mama Tina froze, staring at me, holding the mop aloft.

Commotion rang out from behind us, and four security guards stormed into the room.

"Everyone freeze!" yelled one of the guards.

They clapped Renee, Bindi, and Mama Tina in handcuffs.

I took a deep breath, looking at each woman, then sent an update to Deb and McNearny: *Actually, meet me in the babies' NICU room.*

Renee scooted away from Mama Tina and wailed, "She was trying to kill me!"

"I was not." Mama Tina scowled. "I found you hiding out in a NICU storage closet, and I know the cops are looking for you. I was just trying to keep you here until the police could come arrest you."

I glanced at Mom, who shrugged. "All I know is that that one"—she pointed to Mama Tina—"chased that one"—she pointed to Renee—"into the room with a mop, then bashed her over the head twice." Then she pointed to Bindi. "And that one and I were just protecting the babies."

"Well," I declared, crossing my arms. "I know who the killer is, and she's handcuffed in this room." I studied each woman in turn. "Does anyone want to confess voluntarily? Or should we wait until the police get here and I tell them the story? Voluntary confession goes a long way with a jury. You might get a lesser jail sentence."

All three women squirmed, but none of them said anything.

It didn't surprise me. I gave that speech a lot, and it seemed like criminals never wanted to take me up on it.

"Suit yourself," I said with a shrug.

From her post guarding the babies' incubators, Mom mouthed, "Who is it?"

But I just smiled mysteriously.

The minutes ticked by as we waited for police to arrive. I yawned. *My head feels foggy. I can't wait to go home with my babies.*

My phone buzzed with a text from Rachelle: *How's it going? Should I bring Laurie by the hospital to meet her baby brothers?*

I grinned at the screen and typed, *It's getting late. How about first thing tomorrow?*

Hopefully we'd be discharged at some point tomorrow, and then we could all go home together as a family.

Finally, Deb and McNearny stormed onto the scene together.

"Renee!" cried McNearny plaintively. "Where did you go? I couldn't find you!" Then he noticed the handcuffs and swiveled toward me. "What's going on, Connolly?"

Deb grinned and elbowed him none-too-gently in the ribs. "Looks like she has something for us."

"Connolly?" he asked.

"The killer is sitting here in this room," I said, gesturing down to the three women handcuffed on the floor. "Unfortunately for her, she decided not to come clean when she had the chance."

"Good work." Deb nodded at me. "Let's hear it."

"Three months ago, a newborn died in the NICU as the result of an accident. Anna Jerome."

Tears sprang to Bindi's eyes at the mention of Anna's name. "One of my babies," she murmured.

"She was born full term and healthy, but her mother had gone through a long, difficult labor, and delivery room was chaotic. A nurse tripped and fell while carrying Anna, who sustained head trauma."

McNearny grimaced, sympathy flashing across his features.

I continued, "Like I said, the delivery room was chaotic. The nurse tripped over another staff member—the doula who'd been helping the mom through labor."

Mama Tina looked up sharply.

"It was a tragedy." I pressed my palms together. "But it was compounded by the scheme that Dr. Cory Phillips hatched afterward.

You see, he'd been pocketing a little extra money here and there by doing unnecessary C-sections, but the doulas had gotten in the way. They knew the laboring moms' birth plans, and they advocated for the women in their care. In the inquiry afterward, Dr. Phillips"—I referenced page eight of the report—"told police that he thought Dr. Greene should have done a C-section earlier, that the mom's care had deteriorated because everyone was exhausted, but that the doula had convinced the mom to hold her ground and insist on natural labor."

I locked eyes with Mama Tina. "That doula was you," I said softly.

She nodded slowly. "Yes, it was me. It was a tragedy. I think of that baby a lot."

I stared at her. "You hinted about that baby's death to me," I said, "but you claimed that it happened earlier, and that Samuel had been the NICU doctor responsible for her care. But Samuel's license had already been suspended. He wasn't working as a doctor."

She shrugged, shifting uncomfortably. "I guess I misremembered."

Deb eyed her skeptically. "You misremembered a detail that important? After you tripped up the nurse and got the baby killed?"

"I didn't get that baby killed!" Mama Tina exploded. "It was an accident because the nurse was careless and didn't watch where she was going! Docta C used it as an excuse to get rid of the doulas!"

"Correct," I said. "Docta C told police that he was going to lobby the hospital administration to get rid of the doulas so that an accident like this wouldn't happen again. He convinced Renee and Samuel to back his plan to the hospital administrators, didn't he?"

Renee looked at the ground. "He told me that the doulas were convincing women to ignore the advice of the doctors. I . . . I had doubts, but he told me I was being stupid." She burst into tears. "He told me that he was just looking out for the best interests of the patients."

Deb looked thoughtful. "But that isn't what he told Samuel."

I tilted my head. "What do you mean?"

"You said three months ago?" Deb leaned back against the wall. "Docta C started sending money to Samuel around then, a few hundred dollars here and there. Totaled up to about two thousand in three months. We dug deep into their text messages, and we believe they'd made an arrangement—Docta C paid Samuel a percentage of the extra money he got from each C-section."

I gasped aloud. "So, Samuel testified to the hospital administration for the money." The last piece clicked into place. "Because he didn't make nearly as much as a receptionist as he had as a doctor."

"Plus he had legal bills from the DUI, no doubt," McNearny added with a grunt.

Deb gazed down at Renee. "But we didn't find anything incriminating in his texts to you, and he didn't send you any money."

"That's because she's telling the truth," said McNearny, a sob choking off the last word. "See, Connolly? I was right to believe in her."

Tears sprang to my eyes, leaving my vision misty. "You were," I said softly.

They shared a long, tender look, and then he said, "Get my girlfriend out of handcuffs now!"

The guard uncuffed her, and McNearny ran to her side and engulfed her in an embrace.

"I'm so sorry for freaking out on you, Pat," she whispered. "I've just been so scared and wound so tightly and—"

"Shhh." He kissed her hair. "I know. I know."

Bindi turned a suspicious glare on Mama Tina.

"Renee," I said, "a week ago, you confronted Dr. Phillips about doing too many C-sections."

"Yes," she replied. She rubbed her wrists where the cuffs had chafed. "I'd realized the numbers didn't add up, and that he'd tricked me. It wasn't about the best interests of the patients."

I studied her grimly. "Why did you help persuade me to have a C-section?"

Her jaw dropped. "You . . . the baby was breech! We had to."

"I don't think the baby was really breech," I said sadly. "Docta C texted Samuel about me."

Her nostrils flared. At first, she looked shocked, then rage shone in her eyes. "He promised me he'd be more careful about qualifying patients for C-sections!" she hissed. "He said he'd only do it when there was serious risk. If the hospital started questioning every C-section he gave, it would put patients at risk. It's more dangerous to withhold a needed C-section than—"

"He lied," I said. "Again."

Her face crumpled. "I'm sorry," she whispered. "He said the baby was breech."

"Where were you when you confronted Docta C?" I asked.

She sniffled. "One of the patient rooms, at the end of the hall. Room 150."

"At the end of the hall, you say?" I held her gaze. "Isn't that right near one of the supply closets that the orderlies use?"

She nodded slowly, then the full implication of my words hit her. She whirled on Mama Tina.

"You overheard!" she hissed.

Mama Tina's jaw tightened.

"She did overhear." I clapped my hands once. "And she realized that she—and all the other doulas—had been sacked because of Dr. Phillips's greed." Then I took a deep breath, searching for the right words—this next part was going to be conjecture, but I hoped to provoke a confession out of her. "So she set out to figure out how big this conspiracy really was. She knew that Samuel had also testified that the hospital should fire the doulas. It didn't take her long to find out that he'd done it for financial gain."

"They weren't subtle about it," spat Mama Tina. "All I had to do was time my break to match Docta C's and sit near him in the staff lounge. They didn't outright say it, but after overhearing that conversation with Renee, it wasn't hard to put the pieces together."

"They got you fired, so you decided to kill them," Deb said flatly.

I added, "And I bet when forensics analyzes the note to Renee you so helpfully *found* for us, they'll find that it was in your handwriting, not Docta C's."

Mama Tina clamped her mouth shut. "I want a lawyer now."

"Good." Deb took a step toward her. "You're gonna need one."

CHAPTER TWENTY~TWO

"You are just too precious," I cooed to Primus. "You and your brother! And soon you're going to meet Laurie! Oh, will you all be the very best of friends? I know you will be!"

A NICU doctor finished examining Secundus and turned to me with a pleased smile. "I think they're both ready to go home! Let me get their discharge paperwork ready . . . has Dr. Hobbs discharged you yet?"

I grinned back at her. "My discharge paperwork is in progress."

Just as she left, a knock sounded at the door, and Rachelle walked in, carrying Laurie in her arms.

"Little duck!" I cried. "Mama is so happy to see you! Come meet your little brother!"

Rachelle brought Laurie over to sit next to me, and Laurie reached out to touch Primus's cheek, her little eyes wide with delight.

"Brother," I said, pointing at Primus. Then I pointed at Laurie. "Sister."

"Bada!" Laurie cried. "Bada!"

"That's right! Brother!" I raised Primus's little fist in a victory pump. I looked up at Rachelle. "You can pick up the other baby. The doctor just unhooked him from all the tubes and wires."

Laurie leaned over to give Primus a hug, and I thought my heart might burst.

Rachelle picked up Secundus and kissed his tiny cheek.

It didn't take long for Laurie to get bored and start running around the room, and I closed my eyes and let the tension leave my shoulders.

I solved the case. And now all my children are together, and I get to take them home soon.

Jim entered the room, holding a fast food bag out toward me. My stomach rumbled. "Thank you!" I cried, reaching for it. "Finally something that's not hospital food."

The burger and fries tasted absolutely heavenly. "Can you die of a food coma?" I asked when I finished.

A nurse—not Bindi, she'd understandably taken the rest of the week off—came in with the discharge paperwork for both me and the babies.

"Let's just get this filled out," she said. "What are the boys' names?"

Jim and I looked at each other and burst out laughing. "We . . . haven't decided yet."

"Well, you're not the first. We can just leave this blank for now."

As she continued finalizing the paperwork, Laurie ran up to me and grabbed my leg, and Jim took Secundus from Rachelle's arms.

"You did it, honey," he said.

"*We* did it. Together," I replied. "This case, this family, all of it."

He sat next to me and kissed my forehead. "I'd go on any adventure with you."

I leaned up against him and rested my head on his shoulder, relishing the sensation of his warmth against mine. "And you're the only person I'd ever want to adventure alongside."

"Together," he declared. "Now and always."

I marveled at the miracle of my little family, joy suffusing every cell in my body. "Now and always."

THANK you for reading DOUBLE TROUBLE! I hope you love Kate and her family as much as I do. If you can't wait to read more MATERNAL INSTINCTS MYSTERIES, then keep in touch and let me know! **www.dianaorgain.com**

ONE-CLICK the next Maternal Instincts Mystery – MURDER COMES CRAWLING here!

IF YOU LOVED my MATERNAL INSTINCTS MYSTERIES, you'll love the fast-paced fun of **A FIRST DATE WITH DEATH**. Some are in it for love . . . others for the cash. Georgia just wants to stay alive . . .

AND DON'T MISS my **YAPPY HOUR** Series. It's sweet and funny and you'll laugh out loud as Maggie, not quite a dog lover, hunts down a murderer. Will Maggie's investigation kill her budding romance with Officer Brooks?

AND IF YOU'RE looking for something magical, try **A WITCH CALLED WANDA**. Will fledging witch Maeve reverse the curse that has Chuck doomed to live the rest of his days as a female dog . . . or will someone get away with murder?

SIGN UP at my **www.dianaorgain.com** to find out about new releases and for exclusive sneak peeks of future books. I appreciate your help in spreading the word about my books, including telling a friend. Reviews help readers find books! Please leave a review on your favorite book site.

PREVIEW OF DYING FOR GOLD

CHAPTER 1

"I think your store is haunted," Mrs. Jeffries, one of our best customers, screeched.

"It's not haunted," I said.

"Well, the nugget I was just looking at disappeared out from under my nose! How do you explain that?" she demanded.

"Wendy," I offered as way of explanation, pulling the diamond-encrusted gold nugget out of my sister-in-law's hands and passing it to Mrs. Jeffries.

Wendy simply batted her false eyelashes and gave a wicked grin. "I couldn't resist. Isn't it the most amazing thing you've ever seen?"

The store in question was *The Nugget*. Daddy's family had been part of the original gold rush of 1849. Our family went way back, especially by California standards. I was the fifth generation of a mining family, and *The Nugget* had kept our family in gold even when our mine, *The Bear Strike,* had been forced to close in 1942 to support the war effort.

I don't know that I've ever seen Daddy happier than when the price of gold shot up a few years back and it would finally be profitable to reopen the mine.

Ordinarily, *The Nugget* catered to tourists, but I'd convinced Daddy to use the shop as a backdrop to put my best friend, Ginger's, exquisite jewelry designs on display, and all our best customers and neighbors had come out for the occasion.

Dad came around from behind the counter. "Cut the champagne off," he said under his breath.

I laughed. "Daddy! This is a ladies' gathering. One of the main draws beside Ginger's designs is the champagne."

He leaned into me. "Key word being *ladies*. Do you see how they're acting?"

I couldn't deny that there was a lot of shrieking going on and that the general timbre in the room was reaching an ear-shattering pitch. "You're just mad that they're so excited about Ginger's design and not your gold," I teased.

Dad's idea of jewelry was literally a nugget hanging off a chain, and the chain, of course, must be gold. There was nothing more appealing to him. The rougher the nugget, the more gorgeous Dad thought it was. I had to admit that our regular clientele of tourists seemed to agree.

They loved buying a "gen-u-ine" gold nugget that had been mined from California's oldest and still active mines.

Ginger came out of the back room cradling a sapphire necklace she'd taken to fix that'd been broken a moment earlier when two customers yanked it out of each other's hands. The pendant of the necklace was designed as a huge calla lily with delicate gold leaves and a brilliant-cut sapphire as the blossom. The necklace was almost as beautiful as Ginger herself.

She had honey-ginger colored hair and wore a form-fitting dress that hugged every generous curve. The dress was indigo, and knowing Ginger, it was no coincidence that it perfectly matched both her eyes and the expensive sapphire she now held in her hand.

She stood between the customers, Mrs. DeLeon and Mrs. Harvey, nervously glancing at me. "Uh, Frannie? Can you—"

"It's for me," Mrs. DeLeon said, grabbing at her pocketbook.

"No. You. Don't!" Mrs. Harvey howled. "That piece is for me. Wendy and I have been talking about it for ages!"

All heads turned toward my sister-in-law, Wendy, who dutifully wrinkled her button nose, then admitted, "I did tell her I thought there was a special piece she would like." Wendy avoided Mrs. Harvey's wrath by taking great interest in the passing waiter. "Oooh! Is that pâté?"

We'd hired an upscale catering service, *Bites & Bread*, for the event, and judging by the trays being offered to our customers, I could already hear Dad complain about the bill that was sure to be anything but *bite*-size.

However, he hadn't really had a choice. The competitor caterer was *Golden Grub,* run by mother andafter their horrible divorce, Dad would rather stick himself in the eye with hot pokers than give my mother any business. Plus, he'd said over and over that Mom was just waiting for her moment to poison him…given their animosity I couldn't blame him.

The waiter, who was about all of eighteen, held the tray out for Wendy as Mrs. Harvey took a great inhale, then puffed out her cheeks. She let the air out slowly, breathing all over the canapé tray.

"I'm going to have to speak to Mr. Peterson! George!" she wailed.

Dad appeared with a smile on his face. He was ever the charmer, but I could tell by the fine lines around his eyes that he was tired. One more complaint from the wealthy, pampered socialites this party had attracted and he might blow a gasket.

"Mrs. Harvey. Whatever is the matter? More champagne?" he offered.

I bit back my laugh.

So much for cutting off the champagne!

"George. Will you please inform Mrs. DeLeon that the sapphire necklace is for me?"

Dad grabbed the arm of another waiter, this one a redhead who worked regularly at the *Bites & Bread Bakery,* and pulled a bottle of champagne out of her hand. He topped off Mrs. Harvey's glass. "Sapphire?" He frowned. "Mrs. Harvey. You and I must have a talk." He glanced around, all the ladies suddenly craning their necks to get an earful. "In private," he mumbled, leading her toward the glass case that held our most expensive gold jewelry.

Dad handed me the champagne bottle, then took Mrs. Harvey's elbow, leading her to the back of the store as he chatted with her, tilting his head close to hers so his mouth was near her ear. She suddenly erupted into a fit of giggles, then whacked my father on his shoulder. I noticed her hand lingered on his arm, giving him the occasional squeeze.

Didn't she realize she was the one being squeezed?

Mrs. DeLeon said, "Quick, Frannie. Ring me up for the sapphire necklace so I can get out of here and away from Mrs. Harvey."

I topped off Mrs. DeLeon's flute. "I think she'll change her mind altogether about the necklace. Don't worry."

Mrs. DeLeon handed me her platinum American Express. "I'm not taking any chances."

I took the card and nodded. "It is a beautiful piece. I'm sure you'll be very happy with it."

Ginger beamed as I rang up the necklace. "I can't believe this is happening. Everyone loves my stuff."

"I knew they would. It's beautiful," I said.

Wendy slipped up next to us. "Totally unique," she agreed. "I'm so glad I convinced George to have the party. What a great idea I had!"

Ginger and I exchanged a look. Actually, the idea of hosting an exclusive sale of Ginger's handcrafted designer jewelry had been mine, but we both knew Wendy would take credit wherever she could get it.

I rang up Mrs. DeLeon and placed the beautiful sapphire necklace into a black velvet gift box.

Wendy and Ginger circulated around the crowd, and Dad popped open another champagne bottle while chatting with Mrs. Harvey.

As I finished helping Mrs. DeLeon, she leaned in and grabbed my hand. "When are we going to see a ring on this finger, Frannie?"

I flushed. For some reason, I hated being the center of attention. I'd much rather people notice the sparkling gold nuggets beneath the glass counter than my hand above it.

"It's getting to be about that time, isn't it, dear?" Mrs. DeLeon asked.

I slipped my hand out of her grasp and feigned a smile. Even though I was hoping for a proposal soon, I wasn't about to share the details of my private life. "When he's ready, I'll be ready," I said.

Mrs. DeLeon gave a throaty chuckle. "Well, my dear, don't wait too long. I know your father is dying for some grandbabies to help out with *The Bear Strike*. Speaking of grandbabies, where did Wendy fly off to?" Mrs. DeLeon turned to look for Wendy.

Oh, good. She could go bug Wendy about getting pregnant soon and that would get me off the hook for the moment.

"Over there," I said, pointing toward Wendy's slender form. "No baby bump yet . . ."

Wendy turned toward me as if she'd sensed we were talking about her. I winked and wiggled my eyebrows, indicating that Mrs. DeLeon was about to descend on her.

She gave me her best "you'll pay for this" look, then smiled as Mrs. DeLeon approached.

I took the opportunity to slip to the back and dial my boyfriend, Jason. We'd been dating for almost a year, and he'd recently been hinting around the idea of marriage, asking my ring size and whether I preferred white gold or yellow.

Which actually was a silly question for a gold heiress. While gold could be many colors, including black or purple, nothing compared to those flakes colored like the sun. But hey, if being agreeable to pink or red gold would get a ring on my finger, I was all for it.

In fact, Jason had been mysterious about this evening. He'd mentioned a romantic dinner and a *surprise*.

I dialed his number and waited for him to answer. It rang four times, and then his voicemail kicked on.

Where was he?

It wasn't like him not to pick up.

Maybe he's shopping.

I imagined him haggling with a jeweler across the glass counter. No, that wasn't likely. Surely if Jason was getting ready to propose, he'd have asked Ginger to design the ring. And yet, she hadn't mentioned a thing.

Footsteps approached, and I tried to hide the smile that was bursting through.

Wendy appeared before me. "What are you grinning at? Siccing Mrs. DeLeon on me?"

I laughed. "Oh, Wendy. Sorry. I couldn't resist, plus she was pestering me about when Jason is going to pop the question."

"It better be soon. He'd be an idiot to let you go." Wendy suddenly took a step back and evaluated me. "What style dress do you want?"

I inwardly cringed. Wendy's new hobby was sewing, and she fancied herself a dress designer, but the truth was she barely knew the difference between a straight stitch and a whip stitch.

She grabbed the fabric measuring tape that was constantly slung around her neck these days and moved toward my waist.

I stepped back. "Wait, wait. Let's not jinx anything. It just that he's been hinting around and he's making me dinner and tonight—"

Wendy squealed and wrapped her arms around my neck. "OMG! You'd better call me first thing."

The sound of high heels clicked on the tile floor. "Call you first about what?" Ginger asked.

"She'll call me first after the proposal," Wendy said.

Ginger and Wendy were on-and-off-again friends and sometimes got a little competitive when it came to attention from me. I suddenly found myself in a tug of war between the two.

"She'll call me first!" Ginger said. She quirked an eyebrow at me and said, "Right? I'm her best friend."

Wendy stepped in and put an arm around my shoulder. "Well, I'm her sister-in-law. Family trumps friends; everyone knows that."

Ginger grabbed my other arm. "No. Not true— "

I wrapped an arm around each of their shoulders. "Okay, as soon as he asks, I'll conference you both or"—I laughed—"send you a group text."

Dad popped his head into the back room. "For goodness sake! What are the lot of you doing back here? I have biddies bidding on baubles, ready to overpay and rip each other's gizzards out over these trinkets. Now get out there and close those sales!"

We laughed.

"Great pep talk, Dad," I said.

He ignored our laughter and began to usher us toward the sales floor. "Hurry now, Mrs. Harvey needs to be rung up for the nugget I just sold her."

Ginger looked offended. "But I thought she was interested in the emerald tennis bracelet I designed for her." She scurried off behind Dad.

Wendy and I followed, but she hung back a bit and said to me, "I got a text from Ben." She rolled her eyes. "You'll never believe it, but more changes for Living History Day."

Living History Day was an annual event where the entire town dressed up in 1850s garb that Wendy helped sew. It was a huge fair complete with sawmill demonstrations, tours of famous gold mines, historic reenactments, and gold panning. And, of course, lots of tourist memorabilia and junk food, topped off with a healthy dose of live music.

Our mutual friend, Ben, and his band *Oro Ignited* played every year.

"What's going on?" I asked.

Mrs. Jeffries, still clutching the diamond-encrusted gold nugget, spotted me and waved frantically at the glass counter. "Frannie! Show me those gold coin earrings! I think they'd make quite a match with this knickknack." She wiggled her wrist so the nugget moved back and forth hypnotist-style.

I moved across the sales floor and behind the counter as Wendy followed me.

"His band's been canceled," Wendy said.

I pulled the earrings for Mrs. Jeffries, who was now absorbed in our conversation.

Mrs. Jeffries pursed her lips. "More problems with Living History Day?"

"Problems with Dale Myers more specifically," Wendy answered.

Dale Myers was the new chairman for Living History Day.

"Dale Myers!" Mrs. Jeffries spat. "That man is making so many enemies. Why, I wouldn't be surprised if he winds up murdered! Did you know that my dear Mr. Jeffries and I were all set to sing for the event?"

"Were?" I repeated.

Mrs. Jeffries nodded, her expression changing to resemble that of a moping child. "Dale said that there were already too many acts scheduled and that he'd have to bump Edmond and me off the list. Can you imagine? We've been singing on Living History Day for twenty-five years." She crossed her arms with a huff. "Not a very nice thing to do to us when we've just reached our quarter-of-a-century singing anniversary."

Wendy shook her head. "It's downright cruel if you ask me. Such a shame."

The Jeffries were by no means an act that would make it on Broadway. But they had a familiar, hometown sound and I couldn't imagine Living History Day without it.

"That's strange he would say that there are too many performers," I remarked. "I mean, if you two got bumped off the program and now Ben's band too, we won't have any entertainment."

Mrs. Jeffries looked down at the earrings Wendy had just handed her. "You're exactly right." She released a long-suffering sigh as she held the earrings up so that they sparkled in the sunlight streaming through the window. "I came in here to forget about all this. But Dale Meyers's doom and gloom managed to follow me here too."

Wendy offered a sympathetic smile. "I'm sorry about that. But don't you love those earrings? They're just the thing to cheer you up."

Mrs. Jeffries' face brightened considerably. "Yes.. . . . yes, I think you're right. I'll take them, Wendy!"

I barely hid my laughter at how quickly Mrs. Jeffries was consoled by the purchase. I supposed that it didn't matter what sold Ginger's jewelry so long as the afternoon was a success. Still, Dale Meyers had cast quite a shadow, and it seemed Ben wasn't the only one who was unhappy about it.

PREVIEW OF DYING FOR GOLD

CHAPTER 2

At six p.m., we finally ushered everyone out of the store. Three cases of champagne later, we'd rung in one of our best nights for fine jewelry. Dad was grudgingly pleased, even if gold had taken a back seat to fine stones for one day.

Ginger was beside herself, squealing every three minutes. "We need to go out and celebrate!"

"I have a date with Jason," I said, pressing my hand against my tummy to quell the butterflies.

Tonight could be the big night!

"Right, right," Ginger said. She glanced over at Wendy. The two never went out without me, but it seemed that the day had been so successful that they might be gearing up for it. "Well, do you want to get a glass of Chardonnay with me over at the Wine Jug?"

Wendy shrugged. "Sure, why not? I've tolerated you all day. I might as well tolerate you a little longer." Ginger giggled as if Wendy had been joking.

I pinched Wendy. "Be nice."

Wendy laughed. "Okay, I'm just kidding. Besides we need to be together so you can call us when you get your big news."

I slipped my cell phone into my pocket.

"Don't worry, I'll call you guys. How late will you be at the Wine Jug?"

"Late," Ginger said. "We're celebrating. We're going to be late."

Wendy glanced at her watch. "Well, my darling husband will be home from the mine—"

Ginger grabbed Wendy's arm. "No you don't. If we go to the Wine Jug together, you can't ditch me."

"I'll walk with you guys since it's on my way to Jason's," I said, wiggling my fingers in Dad's direction.

Dad, who was closing down the final till, said, "See you in the morning. Don't stay out too late."

I hadn't exactly told him that I expected Jason to propose tonight. I knew Dad wasn't very fond of the idea of Jason and me getting married. Dad wanted me to marry again, sure, but Jason's career goals were not part of Dad's overall plan. Dad had made it clear that he wanted me to stay in Golden and run *The Nugget*, and Jason was in line for a promotion and the new position included moving to New York City.

As it happened, I personally loved the idea of moving to New York. The Big Apple was glamorous: skyscrapers, fine dining, Fifth Avenue department stores with designer names, theater, and opera.

All we had designer in Golden were secondhand goods sold in a small store around the corner from *The Nugget*. If you wanted to do any real shopping, you had to head down the Sierra foothills and into Sacramento to hit a mall. But even then, it wasn't nearly as sophisticated as New York.

Ginger, Wendy, and I walked the steep and windy streets of downtown Golden, passing the Chocolate Shoppe, the antique clocktower, and the theater. Dusk was falling, and one by one, the vintage lampposts that lined the narrow walkways flickered on.

We stopped in front of the Wine Jug before saying goodbye.

"Call me first thing," Ginger said, pushing open the door to the bar.

Wendy followed her in, but not before turning around and mouthing to me, "Call me first!"

I waved at them and then proceeded up the hill toward Jason's apartment. It was strange that he and I hadn't spoken all day, but maybe it was because he had a surprise in store for me . . .

Like a proposal.

I pushed the thought out of my mind. No need to go overboard with anticipation. If the time was right, Jason would know.

I'd been married before, but only for a short time. We'd both been straight out of high school and considered it a *starter* marriage. At least that's what everyone else called it, I think partly to make me feel better. Being a divorcée at twenty-one is not exactly what a girl dreams about, and it still broke my heart to think about how quickly it all fell apart for us. But things were different now.

This time around it'd be forever.

I turned the corner on Jason's street and climbed the rickety staircase to his apartment. In real estate lingo, they'd call the staircase *original*, but in reality it was one board shy of a full disaster.

I pressed the doorbell, waiting for Jason to answer. After a moment, the door flew open and my boyfriend appeared. There was stubble on his normally clean-shaven cheeks, his shirt was wrinkled, and he looked like he hadn't slept in twenty-four hours.

Ah! My computer genius.

I pressed my lips to his. "What's going on, Jason? You're a mess. Did I wake you?"

He dragged a hand across his blond hair. "No, um, I've been working. You know, I'm focusing on that promotion, so I was . . ." He shrugged his shoulders. "Did we have plans for tonight?"

"Yeah." My heart sank. He'd forgotten our date altogether. So much for a proposal. "I thought we were going to have dinner."

"Oh." He looked befuddled. "Um." He scratched his head. "I think I've got a box of pasta somewhere. You want to have spaghetti and sauce?"

"Hmm. Spaghetti and sauce sounds appetizing," I teased, poking him in the ribs, but he looked more offended than happy.

"Come on in," he said.

I followed him into his apartment. There were papers strewn across his coffee table, and his laptop was open and buzzing.

Jason did a little a jig and rotated his body so that it blocked my view of his screen. He seemed a little jittery.

Why was he acting so strange?

"Are you even hungry?" I asked.

"I could eat," he answered. "You know, I can always eat."

He padded over to the kitchen and waited for me to follow. He pulled open the refrigerator door. There was a half-full bottle of Chardonnay and a carton of eggs. Aside from that, the refrigerator was empty.

"I cleaned out the fridge earlier," he said.

"Do you want to go out to eat?"

"Out?" He suddenly looked ashen. "Uh, you know, I'm working on this project. I don't think I have time to go out. I'll miss my deadline."

"Well, I could fry a couple eggs for us," I said, ignoring the unsettled feeling creeping into my heart.

He rocked from his toes to his heels and then back again. "If you're hungry, that's fine. Or we could order takeout."

Jason was always ordering takeout, the ultimate bachelor. I figured one day when we were married, I'd show him what a regular Martha Stewart I was. I could cook with the best of them. I opened the small cupboard that made up his pantry.

"Let's see if I can find some beans and salsa or something. I'm sure I can make something yummy out of those eggs."

"No, don't bother. It's kind of a hassle to cook." He pulled out the bottle of Chardonnay and poured a glass for me.

"It's only a hassle to cook if you're not hungry," I said.

"I am hungry," he admitted.

"Well, then I'll make something." I rummaged a bit more through his cupboard and came up empty-handed. "If you had some chorizo and peppers, I could make you *Huevos a la Flamenca*."

"I love it when you talk sexy to me," he said, pouring himself a glass of Chardonnay.

I socked him in the shoulder. "It's not sexy, it's Spanish."

"Same thing."

"I guess we'll have to settle for fried eggs. You do have oil, don't you?" I asked.

He pinched the bridge of his nose as if the mere thought of groceries or anything to do with cooking gave him a migraine. "I dunno."

"It's okay. I can poach the eggs." I grabbed a pot and filled it with water as I brought him up to speed on the success of the sale and the overall events of the day. I ended with telling him that Dale Meyers was making life a living hell for the Living History Day.

Jason sipped his wine, then groaned. "Dale's a nightmare. He's making my life miserable too."

"How's that?" I asked.

Jason looked like his thoughts were a million miles away, then he said suddenly, "I've been so busy I probably haven't even told you yet, but my department head got transferred and now I report directly to Dale. It's him who's going to decide if I get promoted or not."

"Oh, Dale's not so bad. I thought you guys got along. Wasn't he the one who hired you?"

Jason was a computer engineer who did his best work uninterrupted. It was sheer misery for him to go into an office and meet with the business team, but once he and Dale met, Dale had arranged for Jason to telecommute, and Jason hadn't stepped foot into the Sacramento branch in ages.

Jason paled. "Yeah. Seems like a long time ago, though. A lot's changed." He suddenly looked depressed.

"Why don't you go work on your project while I fix the eggs?" I suggested.

His eyes lit up. "Oh . . . you don't mind?"

"I'll call you when dinner is ready." I kissed his cheek.

He kissed me back, saying, "You're the best," then disappeared to the front room where his laptop beckoned.

I proceeded to fuss about the kitchen and wipe down the counters with a paper towel. When I went to toss the paper towel, I noticed his garbage was full.

If things went according to plan, soon this would be *our* garbage! Our *New York* garbage!

Oh, who cared if Jason was busy with work tonight. Soon we'd be married. Of that I was sure.

I tied the kitchen garbage bag up and headed down the back steps where the larger trash bins for his apartment were kept: a black one for refuse, a green one for compost, and a blue bin for recycling. All the bins were stationed along the alley next to his apartment building. There was a little trail of dark droplets along the alley that lined up right to the black garbage bin.

Yuk, someone must have had a leaky bag.

I popped open the lid of the trash can and spied a man's shoe.

The shoe might as well have been connected to an electrical current, because it gave me a shock of unmeasured proportions.

What I'd considered to be garbage refuse alongside the trash can I now realized were droplets of blood.

Oh no!

What was a bloody shoe doing in Jason's trash can?

I dropped the kitchen trash bag in the alley and studied the shoe a moment, a thousand thoughts zinging through my head. I grabbed a nearby stick and prodded at the shoe. When I moved it, blood oozed out.

A chill zipped down my spine.

Whose shoe was this?

How did it get here, and why?

Suddenly, a loud bang echoed down the street and the thought struck me that I might be in danger. I slammed down the lid and raced back up the stairs to Jason's apartment.

"Jason," I screamed as I pushed open his apartment door.

He appeared at me side immediately and grabbed my arms. "What's going on? What's wrong?"

I was shaking uncontrollably, adrenaline coursing through my veins. "I went to take down your garbage . . . I . . . there's a . . . and some blood . . . I . . ."

"What? Slow down, Frannie. Calm down." He hugged me to him, the warmth emanating from his body soothing me as I took a deep breath.

"I found a bloody shoe in your garbage can," I mumbled into his chest.

He pulled away from me and looked me in the face. "You found some blood in my garbage can? It's probably from the ground beef I tossed yesterday."

"A shoe. A bloody shoe."

I must not have been making any sense, because he blinked at me, then shook his head.

"Why don't you have a seat, Frannie? Did you fall on the stairs and lose your shoe?"

"No, not *my* shoe!" I sat on his couch and stuck out my Jimmy Choo clad feet. "Someone else's shoe. A man's shoe."

He shrugged. "I don't know. Maybe someone threw away an old shoe."

"It looked new."

He sighed. "Babe—"

"And there was blood on it!"

He waved a hand at me, dismissing my fear. "I told you I cleaned out the fridge earlier. I threw out some ground beef. Probably the blood from that dripped on it or something. Look, I have to get this project done. Why don't you just chill a bit? Have some more wine and relax."

"No! You have to go see. What if there's somebody skulking around downstairs!"

He made a face.

I felt like an idiot. He had work to do, and here I was probably overreacting. Suddenly, my fear was gone, but I still needed to be sure of what I'd seen.

He sat down on the couch and pulled me to him, embracing me. "Babe, you know this promotion is important, right? It's the way we get out of this town and to the Big Apple."

"I know."

He pressed his lips to mine. "You do still want to go with me, right?"

"Of course."

"Will you feel better if I go and check out the bloody shoe?"

I laughed. "You're making it sound like a stupid joke. Remember the one about the bloody finger?"

He frowned.

I rolled my eyes. "It's the one where the girl is alone and she gets the call." I made my voice low. "This is the bloody finger . . . and I'm one block away."

He shook his head. "It sounds like a pretty bad joke."

"It is," I agreed. "The girl gets the call three times and gets more scared each time, and then a guy with a small cut on his finger arrives on her doorstep and asks for a Band-Aid."

Jason buried his head in his hands. "Worst. Joke. Ever."

"I know. It's Ginger's favorite, and she's probably told it a million times since we were kids. Every Halloween especially."

Jason rose from the couch. "Okay, I'll check it out." He made his voice low and dramatic. "The bloody shoe."

He left the apartment, and I paced.

Why was there a bloody shoe in his garbage can? I walked to the front window of the apartment and looked out into the dark street. No one seemed to be around. Certainly no one stalking the building or anything else.

I grabbed my phone and sent a group message to Ginger and Wendy:

NO PROPOSAL YET BUT FOUND SOMETHING STRANGE IN THE TRASH.

Wendy texted back first.

A RECIEPT FROM A FINE JEWELER?

Ginger texted.

A USED NAPKIN FROM THE WINE JUG WITH SOME FLOOZY'S NUMBER?

Before I could reply, Jason came back into the room. "There's no shoe in the garbage, Frannie."

"What? It's gone?"

He shrugged. "I guess so. Now we have the case of the missing shoe."

How could it be gone?

"Are you sure you looked in the garbage can? The black one. It was inside, not on top."

"Yeah, I looked inside. You left my garbage bag in the alley, by the way, and Terrance's cat was already clawing it."

Terrance was Jason's downstairs neighbor.

"Anyway," Jason continued. "Since when do you take out my trash?"

I shrugged, poured the last few drops of Chardonnay into my glass, and shook the bottle, hoping for more. I didn't want to confess that I'd been fantasizing about domesticity, so instead I said, "I was bored."

He crossed his arms. "Sorry I can't entertain you, babe, but you know—"

"I know. The promotion."

He wrapped his arms around my waist and pulled me close to him. "One more week and everything will be different. I promise," he whispered into my ear.

I pressed my cheek against his, the stubble of his beard scratching my skin.

"Why don't you go meet up with Ginger and Wendy? I won't be offended," he said.

"No! I'm not going to leave you alone on a Saturday night!"

He laughed. "Babe. I got my work. I feel like I'm the one leaving you alone. I'll walk you to the Wine Jug."

"You don't have to walk me."

"Are you kidding? I gotta make sure you leave." He chuckled at his joke, but it left me feeling unsettled.

PREVIEW OF DYING FOR GOLD

CHAPTER 3

I screamed as someone grabbed me from behind.

The light in the Wine Jug was nonexistent. Okay, you could see, but barely. I always did better after my eyes had a chance to adjust, but Ginger and Wendy tackled me before that happened.

Ginger giggled. “What are you so skittish about?” she shouted over the band, *Oro Ignited*, which was playing on the small stage in the corner of the bar.

Wendy dragged me to their table and poured me a glass of a local white Zinfandel. The golden hills of California were fast becoming a mecca for small wineries that couldn’t afford the high real estate prices in Napa and Sonoma counties. It seemed that every day a new tasting room was popping up, and we were the happy beneficiaries.

The wine was a bit too sweet for my taste, but it was cold, and I wasn’t in a complaining mood.

“I found a bloody shoe in Jason’s trash.”

Ginger frowned. “Was it an old shoe or what? What do you mean bloody?”

“It was a man’s shoe. New shoe. Expensive. It looked like there were drops of blood on it. I told Jason about it, and when he went to check it out, it was gone.”

Wendy refilled her wine glass. “Who cares about an old shoe? What happened with Jason? Did he pop the question or what?”

I shook my head, suddenly feeling self-conscious.

Ginger reached for my hand. "It's going to happen, honey. Be patient."

I nodded, trying to hide the disappointment that was surging in my body. I swallowed hard, and before tears could come, I decided to change the subject back to safe territory. "The whole shoe thing is pretty weird, huh? I can't believe Jason didn't find it. I have to go look again myself," I said over the music. Suddenly, the band took a break and I found myself still yelling, "Will you come with me?"

My face flushed as all eyes turned toward me. I smiled at the neighboring tables and then sipped my Zinfandel.

The crowd got noisy again, and Wendy leaned in. "You mean go back to Jason's and poke around his trash? No way!"

Ginger flashed me look that I interpreted as she'd go with me later when we dropped off Wendy. I nodded at her, and she winked at me conspiratorially.

Wendy was too delicate to go digging in someone's trash. Even if that someone was my intended, or soon-to-be intended.

"Come on, you're good at digging," I teased her.

"Gold digging maybe." She smiled and batted her false eyelashes at me.

"Or digging for gossip," Ginger added. "She's great at that."

"A girl has got to have special talents in life," Wendy said.

I grabbed a couple of peanuts from the bowl in the center of the table and a strange sensation tingled through me.

What if Jason was in danger?

Ben, the lead singer of *Oro Ignited* and friend to everyone in town, sauntered over to us. "Evening, ladies. Evening, Frannie." He flashed me a strange, shy look that I couldn't interpret, then turned his attention to Ginger. "I heard your jewelry designs are the hottest fad in town." He took an empty chair from nearby, spun it around, and seated himself at our table with his arms and chest resting on the back of the chair.

Ginger grinned as wide as the Cheshire cat. "Who, pray tell, told you that?"

"My Aunt Jeannie was at the sale today. She brought a flashy pendant, and now my mother is scheming to steal it . . . I mean, borrow it from her."

While Ginger made small talk with Ben, Wendy leaned over to me. "So, what's up? Why do you think Jason didn't propose tonight?"

Her question poked at a sensitive part of my heart, and I suddenly felt hollowed out. I would have much preferred to dwell on the mystery of the bloody shoe than the mystery of the missed proposal.

I'd been so sure. All signs pointed to go, and yet . . .

I shrugged and felt my eyes start to fill.

Wendy grabbed my hand. "Oh, honey! Come on." She pulled me to my feet and led me to the ladies' room. Under the fluorescent lights, I looked like the wreck of the Hesperus.

"No wonder he didn't propose! Look at me!" I yelped.

Wendy laughed and smoothed down my hair. "You be quiet. You look fine."

While Ginger had always been my closest girlfriend and had nursed me through my shares of broken hearts, Wendy was a more recent addition in my life. Being that she was married to my brother and we worked together on a daily basis at The Nugget, I was finally starting to feel like I could confide in her.

I collapsed onto the chaise in the ladies' room and sighed. "I'm not giving up. I'm still sure he's the one, but he's under a lot of pressure is all. I think next week, after he gets the promotion . . ."

Wendy ran some tap water and wet a paper towel. She quirked a brow at me as she pressed the towel to the back of my neck. "You can have anyone in town, darling. I don't want you to settle."

I frowned. "I'm not settling! I love Jason."

She nodded. "Of course you do. What about Ben? Have you noticed the way he looks at you?"

I felt a surge of defensiveness. "I love Jason. He's the one."

She dabbed delicately at her lips. "Right. Ben and I were talking earlier. He and I made a deal."

"What about?" I studied Wendy's reflection in the mirror, wondering what was coming next. Ben had been best friends with my first husband, but they'd parted ways more or less about the time of our divorce.

"He wants me to use my power of influence with Dale Myers to get his band back on the main stage for Living History Day."

I snorted. "What power of influence?"

Wendy laughed. "Well, I am in charge of all the costumes. Don't you think the threat of having everyone dance around naked is substantial?"

We giggled. The kind of infectious, delirious laughter bubbling through us after a stressful day was enough for us to slump together and wipe the tears dry.

Taking advantage of her good mood, I said, "Come with me to have a look in Jason's garbage can."

Wendy scrunched up her nose. "I told you. I'm not digging through someone's garbage."

"You don't have to dig through his garbage. I just want to see if the shoe is there." She looked unconvinced, but I laced an arm through hers and pulled her out of the ladies' room. "What are sisters-in-law for anyway?"

"Not this!" she protested, but she didn't untangle her arm from mine.

"I won't tell," I urged.

She snickered. "Your brother would die if he knew I was digging through someone's trash."

"I know, I know. You're a gold digger, not a trash digger," I teased.

She pinched my arm. "Shut it, sister."

I laughed, but she only pinched harder until I said, "Ouch! Okay, okay, I take it back, humorless."

Back at our table, the entire band had joined Ginger for cocktails. She was flirting outrageously with all of them, sitting on someone's lap while another guy rubbed her feet. I knew I'd never be able to convince her to leave with us. Instead, I wiggled my fingers at her in farewell. She made a phone receiver out of her hand and gestured that she'd call me later.

Wendy and I exited the Wine Jug, the cool night air a reprieve from the stifling atmosphere of the bar. We walked down the streets of Golden arm in arm, Wendy chatting about the costumes she was finalizing.

Even though I tried to focus on her chatter, my mind was on the bloody shoe. When we turned the corner to Jason's block, a chill crept up my spine. What exactly was I going to do with the shoe if I found it?

We entered the alley, and a cat hissed at us, then ran off.

A black cat no less.

Wendy screeched, "Bad luck!"

I poked her in the ribs. "Don't worry about that. It's the neighbor's cat." I said it to calm her down, but the truth was I was superstitious too.

The alley was curiously clean. There were no drops of blood like before. It was as if someone had scrubbed the concrete clean.

I flipped open the lid of the black garbage can.

There was no shoe. There wasn't anything, not even garbage.

"How weird! It was here," I said to Wendy.

"Where?" she asked.

"The place is spotless. Garbage pickup isn't until Monday," I said.

"Somebody must have picked it up," she answered.

I looked through the other bins quickly. The recycling and compost bins were half-full and seemed the same as before. "It doesn't make any sense. Does it?"

"No," she said. "It doesn't make sense that you would drag me out here to look at an empty trash can."

I poked her shoulder for her to be quiet, but she was just getting started.

"It's like the time you hauled me over to the Dress Stop to rummage through the sales bins when the sale was already over. Do you remember? Or the time—"

I pulled out my phone and quickly dialed Jason, glaring at Wendy and shushing her as I left a voicemail for Jason.

"He didn't answer," I said. "I'm going to go up and see if he's okay."

Wendy flashed me a look of concern. "Why wouldn't he be okay?"

"I don't know. I'm sure he's okay. That's not what I meant. I guess I'm just freaked out."

She shrugged. "I know you were hoping for a proposal, sweetheart, but sometimes the men, they keep us waiting. Give him some space. Do you know how long it took your brother to propose?"

I wasn't about to get into this conversation with Wendy again, so I said, "Speaking of which, George is probably back from the mine and wondering where you are."

"Right. I'd better go." Wendy wrapped her arms around me and gave me a squeeze. "Walk me to Pine?"

Pine Street was only a short way down the street, and from there we'd head in different directions. We walked in silence, then said goodbye at the intersection. I knew she'd asked me to walk her this way so that she could ensure I'd head home instead of going back to Jason's.

I watched her leave, and when she rounded the next corner, I doubled back toward Jason's apartment. It wasn't worth discussing with Wendy. She didn't understand that I needed to see him again.

I rounded the corner and sat on the steps of his apartment house and called his cell again.

No answer.

He was probably working, and it would be pushy of me to intrude. After all, I'd already called him twice. Still, the matter of the garbage being whisked away was bothering me. What if something had happened to him?

No, I was being ridiculous.

I fidgeted on the stairs, not knowing whether to go up or not. I imagined Jason surprising me at the top of the stairs with a ring. Although he had been rather standoffish tonight, could it be he had a black velvet box hidden somewhere in his apartment and was waiting for the right time to ask me?

He was probably waiting for his promotion. Maybe he'd surprise me with the news of the promotion and then pop the question. Yes, that's probably how it'd go down. Jason would make reservations at the local chophouse for Friday night. That seemed fancy enough. It wasn't New York City fine dining, but at least they had white tablecloths.

Then Living History Day on Saturday; it could be my going away party from Golden. All my friends would be there, and maybe *Oro Ignited* would play after all. I'd be able to say goodbye to everybody in style with a big fat diamond on my hand.

Oh, where was Jason?

I dialed his number again.

No answer.

Forget it. I climbed the steps to his apartment and knocked at the door. "Jason?"

Silence.

He's probably wrapped up in his work.

Still. I had to at least see him one final time before heading home.

My forgetful computer genius kept an extra key under his mat. It seemed that all he could keep track of were formulas and advanced algorithms. Forget about keys and wallets. I unearthed the key, stuck it in the door, and slowly pushed it open.

I peeked my head in. "Honey."

No answer.

I tiptoed into the apartment. It was eerily quiet.

"Jason?"

Still no response.

I walked to the living room; his laptop was still aglow.

Where was he?

He'd probably gone out to get something to eat. Maybe he was at *The Spoon*, our local burger joint, enjoying a greasy cheeseburger and all the fries he could stuff into his face.

I turned on my heel and headed toward his bedroom, still calling out to no avail, "Jason?"

Before I could push open the door to his bedroom, my phone buzzed. Jason's face illuminated the screen. "Hello?" I said into the phone.

"Frannie, where are you?" Jason asked.

"Where are *you*?" I asked.

"I'm at the Wine Jug looking for you."

"Oh! I came back to your place. I was worried about you," I said.

"My place?"

Was I imagining it, or was there a tone of panic in his voice?

"Yeah. I used your key from under the mat. I got worried about—"

"Worried? Uh . . . stay there! I'll be right back," he said.

"Okay."

"Sit on the couch in the living room. I'm coming right now," he said.

"Alright, honey, no problem." The cell phone reception started to get spotty, our connection sputtering and cracking. "I'll see you in a minute," I said, ready to hang up.

"Wait for me in the living room," he said again.

"Right," I agreed.

"My bedroom's a mess," he added by way of explanation.

"Don't worry about that," I said.

Why was he all nervous and panicked? Was he hiding something in there? A black velvet box, perhaps?

We hung up, and I couldn't resist. I pressed my palm against the door to his bedroom and pushed it open.

The room was not messy at all. In fact, it was the opposite of messy. It was nearly empty.

The bed was made and a few file boxes were sitting between the closet and his nightstand, as if he'd been packing.

That was strange.

My stomach flip-flopped, an odd feeling spreading from my torso into my throat. Certainly he was planning on proposing, he was just packing up getting ready for our move to New York. That had to be right. He was packed up to move with me . . . *with* me, not without me.

Right?

I carelessly opened one of his dressers. It was empty—no socks, underwear, or small velvet box.

No!

There had to be a mistake. Jason wasn't going to leave without proposing. He was *going* to propose; we were moving to New York *together*. I knew that.

I slid open the mirrored door of his closet. Two dark suits hung side by side like lost, forgotten soldiers. The rest of his closet was packed up.

I swallowed the dread bubbling up inside my throat.

He was going to leave!

He was leaving me in Golden. He was taking off to New York after the promotion on his own. He hadn't said anything to me about packing.

A mixture of sorrow and rage boiled inside me. I kicked the trunk by the end of bed.

Was the trunk empty too?

Without hesitation, I yanked open the lid. An unexpected sight burned my eyes, and a bloodcurdling scream escaped my throat, leaving me woozy and aghast. Inside the trunk was the shoeless body of Dale Meyer.

To continue…

Click <u>here</u> to get your copy now.

OTHER TITLES BY DIANA ORGAIN

MATERNAL INSTINCTS MYSTERY SERIES

*Bundle of Trouble - FREE*The only thing tougher than solving a murder…giving birth!

Motherhood is Murder Kate joins a new mom group where mischief and murder run rampant.

Formula for Murder A hit and run crash catapults Kate into a mystery at the French Consulate.

*Nursing a Grudge*Kate's budding PI business is threatened when a new PI poaches her client.

*Pampered to Death*Spa day has never been so deadly!

Killer Cravings Can Kate juggle being a PI, pregnant and those cravings all at the same time?

A Deathly Rattle Who shot rival PI, Vicente Domingo?

Rockabye Murder Dancing can be murder—literally.

Prams & Poison Are there too many skeletons in the Victorian closet Paula's is renovating?

LOVE OR MONEY MYSTERY SERIES

*A First Date with Death*Reality TV meets murder!

A Second Chance at Murder Georgia's new boyfriend disappears in the Pyrenees Mountains.

Third Time's a Crime If only love were as simple as murder…

ROUNDUP CREW MYSTERY SERIES

*Yappy Hour*Things take a *ruff* turn at the Wine & Bark when Maggie Patterson takes charge

Trigger Yappy Salmonella poisoning strikes at the Wine & Bark.

IWITCH MYSTERY SERIES

*A Witch Called Wanda*Can a witch solve a murder mystery?

*I Wanda put a spell on you*When Wanda is kidnapped, Maeve might need a little magic.

*Brewing up Murder*A witch, a murder, a dog...no, wait...a man..no...two men, three witches and a cat?

COOKING UP MURDER MYSTERY SERIES

Murder as Sticky as Jam Mona and Vicki are ready for the grand opening of Jammin' Honey until…their store goes up in smoke…

Murder as Sweet as Honey Will the sweet taste of honey turn bitter with a killer town?

Murder as Savory as Biscuits Can some savory biscuits uncover the truth behind a murder?

Building a relationship with my readers is one the things I enjoy best. I occasionally send out messages about new releases, special offers, discount codes and other bits of news relating to my various series.

And for a limited time, I'll send you copy of BUNDLE OF TROUBLE: Book 1 in the MATERNAL INSTINCTS MYSTERY SERIES.

Join now

ABOUT THE AUTHOR

Diana Orgain is the bestselling author of the *Maternal Instincts Mystery Series,* the *Love or Money Mystery Series,* and the *Roundup Crew Mysteries.* She is the co-author of NY Times Bestselling *Scrapbooking Mystery Series* with Laura Childs. For a complete listing of books, as well as excerpts and contests, and to connect with Diana:

Visit Diana's website at www.dianaorgain.com.

Join Diana reader club and newsletter and get Free books here